The Other Side of Side of Her

By the same author:

When Strangers Meet…
That Frequent Visitor

Praise for his work:

"High suspense and entertainment... This young author walks his talks…"

– The New Indian Express

"His characters speak the slang of the places they come from, be it Gurgaon or Chennai..."

– The Hindu

"Storyteller at heart..."

– The Deccan Chronicle

"Once you pick up this book to read, you can't put it down. I bet."

– P.C. Balasubramanian, Author

"…a welcome relief in the midst of many soulless books circulated around and I really liked it."

– Paul Sebastian, Author

The Other Side of Her

HARI KUMAR K

Srishti
PUBLISHERS & DISTRIBUTORS

SRISHTI PUBLISHERS & DISTRIBUTORS
Registered Office: N-16, C.R. Park
New Delhi – 110 019
Corporate Office: 212A, Peacock Lane
Shahpur Jat, New Delhi – 110 049
editorial@srishtipublishers.com

First published by
Srishti Publishers & Distributors in 2018

10 9 8 7 6 5 4 3 2 1

Printed at Repro Knowledgecast Limited, Thane

We lost many loved ones this year.
This book is dedicated to the memories
of the Kerala flood victims.

"Sometimes all it takes is a Stranger's tale to bring your life back on track."

Acknowledgements

I would like to thank editors Lakshmi Krishnan, Stuti Sharma and filmmaker Sangeeth Sivan for their valuable feedback. I would like to extend my gratitude towards Mr. Mohana Krishnan and our beloved aunty from Harippad (who is not with us anymore) for their hospitality and kindness.

There came a point in the recent past when I could not write any further. I had started this book, but could not go beyond the eighth chapter. For almost a year and half, I could not proceed. But all it took was one brilliant song which gave life to the love story of Aarav and Revati, and I was able to start over. The song was none other than *Leilakame* from the Malayalam film *Ezra*. I would like to thank Rahul Raj for composing such a moving song (indeed it moved my story forward).

This book would not have been possible had it not been for Arup & Jayanta Sir – my publishers at Srishti. Big thanks to them.

Without saying, a big chunk of thanks goes to my mother and father for supporting me in my journey as a writer. Above all, I would like to thank God for blessing me enough to write this story.

Most importantly, I would like to thank you… my readers… for picking this book to read. I wish you a good time reading it!

Prologue

The Little Bookshop, Gurugram
23 December 2016

"The most amazing feeling in the world," the bestselling writer, Revati Krishna spoke crisply into the microphone, "*to be in love!*"

The audience, primarily consisting of teenagers, broke into a loud applause.

"It encompasses in one the happiness, the mood, the power and everything you would need," she continued, "Everything you do, you say… Everything you become is defined by that love!"

"People often look for a purpose in their life," she said flipping the penultimate page of her book, "Everyday, you would look up and ask *what is the purpose of my life? What am I doing here? Who are you, God? Are you even there?*," a tear formed in her right eye, "And then God says, from within, *I am the purpose of your life… You are here to seek me… and I am… Love,*" she said closing the book, and wiping away the teardrop that had formed at the edge of her right eye. Her young fans clapped zealously to the scintillating words of their favorite writer.

The twenty-something-year-old emcee picked up her microphone and smilingly said to the writer, "That was awe-inspiring, ma'am," turned to the anticipating fans and announced, "Now, Revati ma'am will be taking questions from the audience."

This was followed by a restless number of hands going up in the air.

"Ma'am, you are known as *the Queen of Romance*, and once again your book has created a huge wave right before release. How does it feel to be in your shoes at this moment?" one of the reporters from a leading women's magazine, sitting in the front row, asked.

Revati remarked without giving a moment's thought, "I think it was your magazine that gave me this title, wasn't it?"

The reporter smiled as Revati continued, "I am happy that my dearest readers are expecting so much from this book, and right now, I feel overwhelmed with the response I have got so far."

"Is it true that the love story is based on a true incident?" the wily reporter inquired.

Revati looked towards the farthest corner of the front row at a middle-aged woman and the man sitting with her. The writer revealed, "Indeed, this story is based on the life of someone I have known very closely ever since I can remember. She has been there for me, throughout my life, my pillar of strength. When my mother passed away, I was only nine. It was she," Revati looked at the woman and continued, "She's my sister, my best friend, Ruchika, who took my mom's place, and made me whatever that I am today. And her love story is the inspiration for this book that I have written."

As the audience tried to take a glimpse of this woman that their favorite writer just talked about, Ruchika blushed and smiled amiably at Revati. Her eyes had filled up too. The man next to her – Vishwanathan Iyer – was her husband. Everyone liked to call him Vishu or Vishu anna. He placed his palm gently on Ruchika's delicate hand.

As the breeze gently caressed the fluttering banner that advertised a welcome note for the writer outside the bookshop, a black sedan arrived. A tall handsome man in a black suit got out of the sedan and walked towards the entrance of the bookshop.

In the bookshop, one of the crazy teenagers was asking Revati a personal question, "Ma'am, I am a huge fan of your books, and I can't wait to read *Love, u n me 4ever*." The fan said looking at the cover of the book in her hand. Her sweet voice reverberated in the ohmic frequencies of the microphone. Revati smiled gracefully, her large dark brown eyes curled at the corners, forming the shape of the petal of a lily. The teenager continued, "Do you really believe that there is something called *true love*?"

"If I did not believe in *true love*, then I would not have written about it."

"Did you find your true love?" the girl asked.

Just then the door opened, and in came the tall man. The door made a jingling sound when the wind-chime hanging nearby welcomed the breeze from outside to pass by. Revati's attention immediately diverted, looking at the man she said, "Yes, I did."

Revati looked back at the teenager and concluded, "People spend ages looking for true love, luckily, mine was right in front of me. Always…"

The man in black suit sat next to Ruchika in the audience. Ruchika smiled at him, her husband shook his hands.

"You are late, Aarav," Ruchika alleged.

"I am so sorry, sis-in-law & Vishu anna, had gone to pick up something from the gift shop for the *love of my life* – The Great Queen of Romance…" he said and his lips parted to make way for a smile that would send any woman rolling up to heaven.

Ruchika nodded her head and chuckled.

"Why don't you ask Revati something?" Vishu suggested to Aarav.

"Hmmm… not a bad idea… let's see…" It didn't take Aarav much time to think what he had to ask, but then he was planning to ask that on another occasion. For the time being he settled with a simpler question.

"What's next? Will your readers get to see something other than romance?" Aarav asked sarcastically.

"Well, I have not thought about it." Revati said with a raised brow. Aarav had always taunted at Ruchika's attempts to write non-cheesy stories with some philosophical value, and he wanted her to write something that was not about love or romance. Knowingly, Revati suggested, "And even if I do, it will essentially be… An Undying Love Story…"

"Does that mean that we will never be able to see the other side of you?" he asked tauntingly.

"Let time be the judge of that…" The writer responded with a smile on her face.

As they walked out of the bookshop, Revati held Aarav's hand and smiled pleasingly. Ruchika and Vishu were right behind them.

"I thought you were not going to make it," the writer told her boyfriend.

"No faith in your *true love*, eh?" Aarav replied winking at Revati.

"Grow up, Aarav!"

As the couple was about to hold each other's hands, a voice interrupted from the back, "Autograph please!" said Vishu as he waved a copy of Revati's book in front of her, "I should get the signature before we leave or else we will forget it like the last time."

Revati took the book from her brother-in-law and started signing it with her fountain pen, "I should rather be punished for delaying the formality that should have been carried out long back."

"That's okay dear," said Ruchika in her gentle voice, "My husband here is more excited to read what all crap you have written about us in your story. You know… since no one else would dare to make this man the *hero* of a novel, and that too a romantic one."

"Oh come on, Didi." The writer eyed her brother-in-law, "Jiju is not that bad."

"Exactly," Aarav said, "He should be given an award too."

"What for?" asked Ruchika.

"For staying with you for so long," Aarav turned to Vishu and winked, "Hats off mate!" Aarav and Vishu exchanged hi-fives and chuckled as Ruchika pinched her sister's lover on the arm.

"Anyway, we should get going now. Our train leaves at six," Ruchika said looking at her red strapped wristwatch.

"Couldn't you stay a little longer?" Revati requested.

"I wish I could, but I have an important workshop at college tomorrow."

"Aarav and I will drop you," Revati offered courteously.

"I think Aarav has more important things to do," she said mischievously looking at her sister's lover.

"What important things?" Revati asked curiously, she noticed Aarav covering his face with his hand in an effort to hide the thief-like grin.

"Our cab is already here. We will see you soon," Ruchika said and rushed towards the yellow cab with her husband.

The couple got inside the cab and moments later, they were waving goodbyes as their cab sped towards the highway.

Revati Krishna's fans were trying to get a glimpse of their favorite writer, some wanted selfies with her.

"Your fans are waiting for you. Just do your thing and we will leave after that," Aarav said in the most supportive tone a man could have for his woman.

"I am worried."

"Why?"

"You know why. I am not sure if your parents would even like me."

"Stop thinking so much. I will take care of that. Just make sure you don't get late because I have promised to reach on time for dinner."

"It's a make or break situation, isn't it?"

"Do you love me?" Aarav asked.

"What kind of a question is that?"

"Just answer my question." Aarav asked piercingly, "Do you love me?"

"Yes."

"Then have faith in your love."

Revati smiled as she looked into his beguiling brown eyes.

"Now, just go and finish off the signing and get done with those selfies," he said pushing her towards the swarm of teenagers who were anxiously waiting for her.

As she walked towards her fans, Aarav realized the challenge that lay in front of him. It was not about convincing his parents about his choice to marry a woman who was from a different community and three years older than him. It was about convincing the woman that he was the right man for her. He slipped out of the scene and lit a cigarette. He watched the puffs of smoke going up in the air, just like his matrimonial worries.

Rising with the smoke… Falling with the ashes…

5:50 pm
Delhi-Jaipur Highway, Gurugram

As the black sedan sped against the wind on the smooth highway that went on till Pune, a nervous Revati joined her palms and prayed, "Oh God! Please please please, take care of everything. I promise I will not eat chicken for a whole year if you… no wait," she stopped to think and then changed her terms, "a whole week! No chicken for a week if you make this work for us."

"You know," said Aarav, "talking to your own self is the first symptom of madness." He mocked his lover's efforts to establish communication with the divine.

"Shut up! You know I am not *talking* to God. Just praying."

"Denial! That is the second symptom," he added and chuckled.

"Can I expect any maturity from you?" she alleged.

"You are older than me, you can handle my little immaturities." Aarav opined.

"Now, I can't change that truth. Can I?"

"We can't go back in time and ask your parents to delay their plans to have you," Aarav said and broke into a silly laugh.

"Gosh! Aarav, could you ever be serious about anything?" the bestselling author asked annoyed by her boyfriend's sense of humor.

"Of course, I am serious…" he paused to look at her, "about you."

"Oh really?"

"Really."

"Can you prove it?"

"Why don't you open that glove-box compartment and see for yourself." Aarav instructed and then turned his face ahead towards the road.

Revati instantly pulled the latch and the small compartment opened. Under the reddish twilight she could only see something spherical inside, wrapped with what seemed like a red ribbon. Revati pulled out the spherical thing as she looked at her lover.

"Maybe you will do better with the lights on," Aarav said and switched on the light inside the car.

As the light fell on the object in Revati's hand, and her eyes caught the first glimpse of the object, her eyes started filling up. It was a snow-globe with a miniature man and woman in bridal outfits, holding each other's hands. The miniature couple was standing on a raised platform.

"You & Me, forever…" Revati read what was written on the platform. Her eyes gleamed with tears of joy.

"I know this is not a huge thing but just a small proof that I want this to be us… forever." His manly voice quivered as it touched a lower pitch.

"This is so beautiful!" she exclaimed.

"Whenever you will miss me, if ever I go away from you… just hold this in your hand and you shall see me holding you closer to my heart," said Aarav.

"I am never letting you go away from me."

"Well, you never know what could happen in future," as he paused to look at his lover whose eyes had already filled up to the brim. He gently caressed her cheek and said, "If something happens to me…"

But before he could finish what he was saying, a speeding truck appeared right in front of them, charging towards them uncontrollably. Revati screamed as she looked at the truck closing in towards their sedan, dropping the snow globe on the floor.

And the snow globe hit the floor, sending the small white particles into chaotic commotion, which slowly settled down over the miniature lovers like flowers falling on a grave…

6 p.m.
Delhi-Jaipur Highway, Gurugram

Revati timidly opened her eyes to the gentle breeze that brushed by her silky hair. She felt a cold sensation ascending from her gut. She turned to see Aarav, who was consciously holding on to the steering. She quickly glanced back and saw the truck fading in the distance.

"What? You thought we had hit the truck?" Aarav asked as he gently parted his lips to speak, "We are alive!"

Revati who was shocked at seeing the approaching truck started punching on Aarav's shoulder to hide her embarrassment.

"Hey, don't do that. I might not be able to save us the next time."

"Shut up!" she scolded her lover. She recollected what he had said right before the brakes had screeched and continued scolding him, "Why do you have to say all those things, huh?"

"Say what?"

"If this was a book, then the reader will have to go back to the last part of the previous chapter to know what you had said."

The writer shrugged as she looked towards the road in front of her and spoke calmly, "I can't think of spending a moment in this world without you. I don't show it, but you know it."

"Neither can I, Revati…"

Revati eyes fell on the snow globe that had fallen below the seat. She bent forth and picked the little piece of memory and looked at it with moist eyes. The snow in the globe had settled on the little couple. She gently shook it, and then the snow unsettled, and the couple was seen again.

She wondered if she could find anybody more perfect than Aarav; the man was tall, good looking, decent, would do anything to make her laugh and when the time came he would take up the role of a responsible man. She always scolded him for being immature, but she knew very well that he just does that to bring that priceless smile on her moon-like face. She felt relieved, and all the worries about impressing and convincing his parents simply faded away into the rainy air that had enveloped the surrounding.

He looked at her without saying anything. His eyes spoke a thousand words, and her dewy eyes, that sparkled under the light of the moon, heard all of them. And then he smiled at the woman he loved, reassuringly.

"I'm there for you… always…" his eyes had said.

8 p.m.
Aarav's house, Mayur Vihar

As soon as she heard the sound of an approaching car, a little girl looked out of the window through the parted curtain. Happiness bloomed on her face as she saw Aarav and Revati arriving in the sedan.

"They are here!" She ran towards the older woman sitting on the sofa.

"Go inside and tell them," the old woman instructed the little girl as she herself started walking towards the window. She alleged as she looked towards her husband, "He had said that he would call me before crossing the metro bridge, we are hardly ready for this!"

Her words did not move the oddly shaped old Mr. Sharma. He was busy enjoying his *roshogola* and *samosa*.

"Why are you always munching on one thing or the other? Can't you stop eating for some time?" his wife scolded him.

"Oho! What happened now?" he asked in a disconnected manner.

"They are here, that's what!"

"Who are they?"

"Are you serious, Prakash Sharma?" the old woman asked as fumes of rage puffed out of her ears.

"No… no, I am not serious. I am in good health, thank God!" Sharma said casually.

"Aarav and Revati are here. Just stop munching on that roshogola!" Mrs. Sharma ordered.

"What does this poor roshogola have to do with my son and the elderly woman he loves? They can wait till I finish."

"Just get up!" Mrs. Sharma snatched the sweetmeat and put it back on the plate. She held her husband by the left hand and dragged him towards the door.

"Why did I ever agree on marrying a Bengali? My dad had warned me the day I told him about you that if I marry a Bengali then she will make me dance on her fingertips. I should have listened to him!" Sharma accused his wife playfully.

"Did I ask you to come after me? Did I ask you to stalk me wherever I went for six months until you had the guts to ask me out for a movie? And what a terrible movie it was – *Don*! *Chee…* I haven't forgiven you for that yet!"

"Firstly, don't you dare say anything about my Big B, and secondly, the only good thing that came out of you was that idiot son of ours and these delicious roshogolas," he glanced towards the half-eaten Bengali delicacy on the plate and complained, "And now you are not even letting me have that."

"Enough for today's insulin shots! Now, please be decent. I don't want the girl to feel embarrassed because of your ways," Mrs. Sharma requested with conjoined hands, "She's a writer, so she is also supposed to be of the intelligent sorts…"

"Surely you are going to have a tough time dealing with such a daughter-in-law."

"Could you stop irritating me? Or do you find enjoyment in doing that?"

"I just love the way you start fuming, and then I get to console you and then," suddenly Sharma molded himself into the shoes of a romantic hero of the eighties, and he caught his wife's arm and pulled her extremely close and whispered, "I get to feel the sweetness masqueraded underneath this spice of a woman."

Mrs. Sharma blushed as her dusky cheek turned red, not with rage but with love. She gently kissed her husband on the cheek and turned towards the door, *"Tum pagal ho, tumhara beta bhi pagal hai!"* she said in accented Hindi and continued in her native Bengali, *"Ekdom Paagol!"*

Outside Aarav's house

Aarav came and took his sunglasses from the car's glove-box. Revati had stopped the moment Aarav had taken an about turn towards the car. Her feet were trembling. Nervousness had taken over the beautiful peach color of her fair face.

"I don't think I can do this," the nervous writer clarified.

"Then I should probably look at that alliance which my aunt was talking about. You remember that air hostess from Gurgaon, right?" Aarav taunted playfully.

"Given your level of maturity, you definitely don't deserve a woman of intellectual depth," Revati shot back at the young man.

Aarav kissed her on the forehead gently and blinked his eyes in a gesture of consolation, "Everything will be alright, just have faith in me... in true love..." he gave a benign smile.

"What if..."

"Shh..." Aarav placed his finger on Revati's rose coloured balmy lips and reminded her, "Just don't forget the protocol. The moment they open the door, fall on their feet like a typical

Indian *bahu*, my mom would love it. Dad is easy, tell him you love roshogolas, and he will be on your side."

The comment made the nervous writer chuckle a bit. She knew that things would be alright because she loved Aarav more than she loved herself; from what she had been writing all these years in a dozen novels, if there is one thing that triumphs in the end – it is true love. And Revati had found her true love in Aarav.

Aarav blinked at Revati and pressed the door bell, and even before the cuckoo could coo, the door opened and the old couple appeared before the younger one. Revati had seen Mrs and Mr Sharma in selfies taken by Aarav, but this was the first time they were standing right in front of her. Aarav touched his parents' feet and gestured Revati to follow protocol which she had momentarily missed.

"Mom, Dad… this is Revati. Remember, I had told you about her," Aarav introduced his lady love to his parents.

Mrs Sharma turned and went inside without saying anything. A gleam of helplessness loomed over Revati's face. She looked at Aarav who nodded casually.

"Do you like roshogolas?" asked Mr Sharma in an artless manner.

"Huh?" expressed Revati as she turned her face towards Mr Sharma and nodded in agreement, "Yes, I love roshogolas!"

"Great, so come inside and help me finish that big bowl of fresh roshogolas before dinner!" the old man opened up heartily.

Realizing how easy it was to woo his father, Revati smiled and almost stepped inside Aarav's home when Mrs Sharma's voice stopped her, "No! Stop right there, Revati. You can't enter this house…" the woman said from inside.

Revati turned towards Aarav anxiously. Had his mother rejected her at first sight?

As Revati took her steps back, Mrs Sharma came out to the door. She held a silver tray in her hand. She continued, 'You are coming to our house for the first time, and I can't let you enter without performing an *aarti*… After all, Goddess Lakshmi must be welcomed properly," she turned to her son and remarked, "Right, Aarav?"

Aarav smiled as he watched his mother light the lamp on the tray and apply the vermilion *teeka* on Revati's forehead. As the older woman's pale finger touched Revati's skin, she immediately felt a rush of gentle breeze flowing through her veins.

"Now, you can come inside, my dear," Mrs Sharma welcomed her son's girlfriend into their sweet abode.

A smile bloomed over Revati's floral face, and as she walked into the hall, a little warm hand held hers. Revati looked down to find it belonged to the angelic little Kriti. Her eyes gleamed in surprise, for she had no clue as to what *her* niece was doing in her boyfriend's home.

"I missed you shoo much, Maasi!" the little girl exclaimed pleasingly.

"I missed you too, but… but what are you doing here?"

"Well…" came a woman's thicker voice, "since it is a happy occasion, we thought we shouldn't miss it."

Revati turned around and saw Ruchika and Vishu standing next to each other.

"What the…" Revati stammered.

"Don't look at us, Revati," Vishu pointed his finger towards Aarav and alleged casually, "It was his plan."

As she turned back to look at the accused she was taken aback. The true love of her life, Aarav, had gone down on one knee, and was holding out a small opened box which had a sparkling platinum ring deeply seated in it. Aarav slowly took Revati's right hand in his.

"Three years ago, I accidentally stepped into my university library where a gorgeous looking writer was launching her book. The moment I saw her; my whole world had stopped, along with my heartbeat, that took a pause. It was love… love at first sight! We became friends and over time, I realized that our feelings were mutual, and when two hearts are destined to be together, then it is called *true love,* and nothing can come between two souls who are made for each other – age, caste, religion, distance… nothing matters!" Aarav stopped to look at Revati's gleaming eyes. The saffron rays of the setting sun were falling on the sea of black that were her eyes, carving a celestial serenity in them.

He continued, "And now, the time has come to take that big leap of faith. Revati Krishna…" he took a gush of air and proposed, "Will you marry me?"

Revati had always written about that perfect proposal and that perfect moment, but never had she imagined that the moment would come in her life for real. All the men from her stories came together in one frame and she realized that she had always pictured Aarav in her stories. This was not just a story, this was reality. The man in front of her was holding out the ring and waiting for her answer. His dark brown eyes were dewy, and so were hers. The tiny specs of hair follicles on her body rose in euphoria, for this was the moment she had always waited for.

"Yes, I will," Revati said and tears of joy streamed down her eyes.

Aarav pulled out the ring and pushed it down her ring finger with a handsome smile on his face. As Aarav and Revati looked into each other's eyes, everyone else looked on gleefully. Ruchika held her husband's hand and took Kriti by her side. Mrs Sharma was happy that his son had finally found the love of his life. Aarav's father felt proud of his son for Aarav had done exactly what he had done years ago while proposing to his mother, Shwornolata Mukherjee Sharma.

Revati said in a hushed tone, "I love you, Aarav."

"I love you too…" Aarav got up and wrapped his arm around Revati, emotions brewing like a drizzle in winter, he whispered into her ear, "You, Me… Forever…"

29th March 2017
Hiranandani Hospital, Mumbai

Dr Pragya gently moved the transducer on Revati's protruded belly. As the transducer rubbed against the gel on the surface of her skin, an image started appearing on the monitor – the image of a little foetus.

"Congratulations Revati, you are going to be a mother!" Dr Pragya conveyed the good news to the nervous writer. As her eyes started filling up with tears, Aarav looked at her compassionately. He took his wife's right hand in his left and their hands conjoined in a warm embrace.

"I hope it is a girl," Aarav stated his desire in a blushing tone, "So that she can be as beautiful as you."

"Unfortunately, I will have to keep you waiting until next year," the doctor said and smiled at the pregnant writer.

"Of course!" Revati replied calmly, although her mind was revolting against the law that made identification of the foetus an act of crime in the country.

As he held his wife's hand, hundreds of questions started popping in his mind, some were pessimistic while others were not. He wasn't sure if he was ready to be a father, but he knew that Revati was smart enough to take care of the two subsequent babies – himself and their unborn child.

While a stream of saline water rolled down from her eye, Revati felt a tickling sensation in her stomach, which probably was the movement of her unborn child. Revati felt like a woman – the potential into which the Creator manifested himself to propagate the evolution of species.

The young couple walked out of the hospital building with a joyous contentment as they held each other's hands and went inside their car.

"I hope you are happy, Aarav," Revati said in a hushed tone.

"Trust me, I am the happiest man on this planet at this moment in time. What are your odds against that?" Aarav stated his contentment in his usual playful manner.

"I am glad. It is just that I was a little worried…"

Aarav started his car and as they passed through the mild traffic on JVLR, he asked, "Worried about what, Revati?"

"Remember what that astrologer in Gurugram had said while calculating the *muhurat* for our wedding?" she pitched in a semi-anxious tone.

"Revati… you know that half of the things that they say are ridiculous and they do it just to churn out money from innocent and ignorant people like our parents."

"Yes, but there are certain things that can be true."

"It is just probability… mathematics, you know. It could be one of the things that *might* happen… and it can happen to anyone!" Aarav tried make his point clear.

"So, the thing he said about not having a baby for two years…"

"Exactly… he had said that we will not be having a baby until two years after marriage. But look, we are having one in just four months. Let's not confuse biology with astrology."

"Yes… but what if…" Revati deliberately stopped her thoughts because she didn't want to imagine the worst that was popping up in her mind, and the very fact that the astrologer who had come to decide their wedding date had seen some obstacles in her horoscope. He had foreseen some trouble with her planetary positions. He had said that if Aarav married Revati, the married couple would not have the good fortune of parenting a baby for two years. This had got Revati worried but she had forgotten the incident until this day when the gynaecologist conveyed the 'good news' at the hospital.

"You are just thinking about nonsensical things right now. Come on, Revati, we should be celebrating, shouldn't we?" He paused to put on his aviator glasses and after that he joked, "You know I would like to name my child Rajini if it's a girl, and if it's a boy, we will tail a *kanth* to the Rajini."

"Mmm…" hummed the writer dejectedly, ignoring the desperate joke of the husband.

"How was your skype call with filmmaker Anuraj Kashyap?" Aarav tried to change the subject.

"I tried to pitch in my love stories but he said that he is looking to make a thriller in Hindi or Tamil with a female protagonist!" Revati said with a drooping face. She sighed and added, "I think I am having a terrible time. Nothing is going my way!"

"Revati…" he turned towards his wife and pressed his right

hand with his left and consoled her, "Don't look back at such unwanted incidents. We have a whole new life ahead – "

Right then a speeding bus crashed right into their car, and the four wheeler tossed and turned over the bridge and into the Powai lake. The car sank into the blue water of the lake as shocked people gathered and looked at the tragic action from above.

The car went down, just like her dilemma. Just like her dreams, it went down.

28th November 2017
South City -2, Gurugram

Revati woke up to the subtle sound of Aarav's breath. She could feel the warm air from his heart whispering into the pores of her soft skin.

"It is a beautiful morning, baby." He said into her ear.

She opened her eyes, but was unable to speak. The words wouldn't come out of her mouth.

Aarav continued, "Shh… it's okay baby. You don't have to say anything… to anyone. I can hear your soul speak."

He kissed the back of her neck and she turned around on the bed only to realize that it had just been another dream, for the love of her life had left her nine months ago. Her eyes filled up as she looked at Aarav's photograph framed on the wall, right in front of her. The sluggish rays of the gloomy morning sun paved through the window and glorified the photo with a morbid sadness. She slowly rose from the bed and walked towards the bathroom.

As she stood in front of the mirror, staring at the scar left on the right cheek, the visuals of whatever she could remember from that gory accident flashed in her mind. She was happy that day, but anxious at the same time, little did she know that the element of coincidence would fail her husband's faith by making the astrologer's prediction come true. The last she could remember was Aarav grabbing her right hand and the speeding truck scrunching up their car in the middle of the highway. She had woken to the tinkling sounds of the surgical instruments and the claustrophobic whiteness of an operation theatre. She helplessly lay on the bed trying her level best to raise her hand that seemed numb to the core of her brain that was keeping her consciousness alive. As the sounds started becoming more sensible to her ears, she realized that the doctors were operating on her body that had been battered in the accident. And then she heard the surgeon tell his assistant, "We will have to save the woman, the baby hasn't survived. Remove the aborted foetus."

That was nine months ago. She was bound to a wheelchair for two months, and held on to crutches for the next four weeks. It was only her strong willpower that made her stand on her feet and walk again. However, the memories of the man whom she loved refused to let go as it overpowered her willpower. Her greatest strength had become her biggest weakness.

Revati walked to her writing table. As she unfolded her laptop, the light of the morning sun fell on the glass of water that was kept next to the machine. She switched on her Lenovo laptop and waited for the sleeping device to wake up. She saw the reflection of her withered face on the glossy screen and ignored the fact that she looked at least fourteen years older than she had looked nine months ago. She opened the draft of her new book that was lying on the desktop and scrolled down to the eighth chapter. The writer tried to frame a sentence but was immediately forced to hit the backspace by her wavering mind. She stared outside the window that was right in front of her trying to ingest some kind of motivation to write, but she could hardly concentrate. She constantly typed something gibberish and embraced the backspace shortly thereafter, thus becoming a pattern often recognized with the writer's block syndrome. As her agony grew into frustration, she banged on the keyboard, sending a key off the grid to the floor. The glass of water also fell off the table and shattered into pieces.

Mrs Sharma came into the room upon hearing the sound of the shattering glass.

"What happened Revati? Are you okay? Did you hurt yourself?" Mrs Sharma asked anxiously.

Revati did not reply, she simply stared at the computer screen. Mrs Sharma picked up the key that was lying on the floor and placed it on the table next to the laptop.

"Revati…" the mother-in-law gently kept her hand on Revati's shoulder.

Revati turned to look at Mrs Sharma's face and burst into tears.

"I can't do this, Maa. I have lost it. No matter what I try, I end up thinking about that day," she cried and sobbing she said, "I don't want to live, Maa. I don't have life without Aarav. He had promised that he won't leave me ever. Why Maa, why did he have to go?"

Poor Mrs Sharma had no answer to the grieving questions of the heartbroken writer. She had been seeing Revati failing to write even a single word in the past few months. In the beginning she had thought that Revati would overcome this phase with time but it was only getting worse with every day that passed.

"*Beta,* I think you need help. Please listen to me this one time. I know you do not like the idea of seeing a psychiatrist, but please let me fix an appointment with Dr Lakshmi."

"Maa, I will be alright, I just need more time. It is normal for a writer to hit a block in her career at some point," Revati pleaded knowing for a fact that she is due by over six months to submit her next book's manuscript to her publisher in Delhi.

"It has been too long now. Besides, Lakshmi is Aarav's aunt. Just consider it like meeting a relative. Please do this for me… Do this for Aarav. Had he been alive, he wouldn't have liked to see you this way," Mrs Sharma begged.

"He's not coming back, Maa. How does it matter what he would have thought now?"

"Please, Revati."

"Okay, I will see Dr Lakshmi," she agreed while wiping away the tears from her face.

Revati knew that this would relieve her mother-in-law for the time being. Besides she also wanted to move beyond the eighth chapter in her book. She was stuck on that chapter for nine months now.

1st December 2017
Dr Lakshmi's clinic, Khan Market

Revati anxiously scratched the surface of her left hand's thumb with the nails of her right hand, as she tried to open up in front of Dr Lakshmi.

"… I have always told myself not to get worn away with the awry challenges that life throws at me. I have advocated the power of being optimistic and determined at all points in life in every book that I have written. But for the first time in my life, I am facing a situation from where all I can see is blankness, all I can hear is silence, all I can think is about that day in the car when I lost the love of my life."

"You have to let go of memories that are holding on to you in order to make space for the ones that are waiting to enter your life. You are blocking your future by sticking to the past in your present," offered the wise doctor, "Try to understand one thing – he's not coming back!"

Revati's face drooped in mourning like a flag in half-mast. Dr Lakshmi had been treating patients with traumatic depression for over three decades now. She placed her hand on Revati's palm and looked at her assuringly.

"Revati, I can understand the phase that you are going through. Getting married to the person you love, expecting a baby and then losing your love and your baby to an accident; it is a traumatic experience for any normal person. Everything here in this city will remind you of Aarav, and it will suffocate you mentally."

"Everyday exposure to negativity in the media will further add to your stress. There is no cure to such negativity but only prevention. Medicines will not help all the time, and I will never suggest medicines to you. Anti-depressants are for those who cannot put up a fight with their inner demons. You, my dear, are strong and intelligent. I would suggest you to take a break from this city. Go to a far-away place, soothe your mind, start working on your novel."

"I am… I don't know. I can't think of going to some strange place and living in a hotel with unfamiliar people around. I have always written in a cosy place and by that I meant home," Revati opined.

"Why strange place with unfamiliar people?"

"I didn't understand."

"You can go to Ruchika's place. I heard from your mother-in-law that your sister moved to a hill station in Kerala. Why don't you go there? It is a peaceful place, and usually people with depression are advised to go to hill stations. You are a writer, you should know!"

"I… I haven't gone there in eleven years," Revati said, "I went there once after Ruchika got married to Vishu anna. It was their reception party."

"Perhaps it is time to go back and refresh those memories," the doctor suggested.

"I will talk to Ruchika," she said and started getting up.

"I will prescribe some medications only for emergency, just to keep you up and going." The doctor etched something on the prescription and handed it over to Revati.

She looks at the medicine's name and asked, "Prozac-22? Is this safe, doc?"

The doctor nodded, "Absolutely!" she said, "But you must cut yourself from this life for some time. From today onwards you will not read or watch news on TV or the internet or any such places. The media highlights negative news to make money, but it creates fear psychosis and hatred in the minds of even normal viewers. Best way would be by getting rid of that smartphone or at least keeping your thumbs away from it as much as possible."

"I hardly use my phone these days." Revati informed.

"Well that is good then. Also, try Yoga and meditation when you feel stressed. It will help you gather your mind." The doctor advised.

"Thanks, I will try it." Revati forced a smile before turning around to leave.

As Revati was opening the door, Dr Lakshmi called her out from behind and remarked, "You know, love is the most powerful healer. Even the greatest wounds can be healed with love. And like any medicine, if you let it overpower you, then it might be the greatest poison. You can fight this, Revati."

Revati smiled and then left the room.

15th December, 2017
Walayar Checkpost, Palghat

As the old Ambassador car passed by the popular Malabar Hotel, the smell of cinnamon sticks and bay leaves crept inside, filling the nasal paths of little Kriti to the extent that her mouth watered for some of their delicious fish biryani. Kriti was a carbon copy of Ruchika in every aspect but when it came to eating habits, she was daddy's girl. Being a vegetarian, Ruchika found the smell of fish biryani suffocating.

"Amma, can we stop here and have biryani, please?" The little girl who was sitting in the front seat next to the driver, requested with beady eyes.

"Little girl, I have told a hundred times, if you eat animals, the animals will eat you someday. Do you want karma to punish you like that?" Ruchika used her usual reasoning which was another desperate attempt to change her daughter into a vegetarian like herself.

"*Maasi*, do you like fish biryani?" Kriti turned to Revati and asked, hoping to hear a yes.

However, Revati did not respond at all. She was lost in her own world. She just kept staring outside the window. The little girl was disappointed. She started playing with the radio's knob. The driver quickly glanced at the activity of the girl's fingers and then got back to driving. Kriti stopped when she heard one of her favorite songs on the radio. The song ended and was followed by news broadcast. Kriti prepared to change the channel when Ruchika stopped her. Kriti frowned and sat on her seat with folded hands.

'Prime Minister Modi signs a monumental pact with Benjamin Netanyu marking the solidification of a strong bilateral relationship with Israel,' the newsreader read in her monotonous voice.

'ISRO will be sending its first manned mission to moon in 2019 and preparations are on the way for India's first astronauts.'

'After filing a fresh mercy plea before the president, Yakub Ali, the accused in the…'

The impatient little girl changed the channel to another one where she could hear songs and not boring news.

This action on the part of the daughter enraged Ruchika.

"How many times have I told you that changing channels without asking is bad manners?" Ruchika asked her daughter.

"Amma! If I don't get to eat biryani, then you don't get to hear the news!" the little girl announced, "And besides, you can always read or watch the news on your phone!"

"Velu, can you please switch off the radio!" a furious Ruchika ordered her driver.

The driver silently turned it off, looking at little Kriti who burst into tears. The little girl clenched her fists and threw a tantrum that brought Aunt Revati out of her trance.

"Kriti, I will take you to the biryani place and we will have fish biryani later, okay?" Revati offered her niece.

"Promise?" the girl asked sulking.

"Promise!" the writer gave her word.

That temporarily drew peace between the mother and daughter. Ruchika clearly did not like the idea of succumbing to the wants of her eight-year-old daughter. She would never want her daughter to even go near the picture of an unhatched egg, let alone eat Kentucky Fried Chicken.

"So, what are you writing about these days?" Ruchika tried to start a conversation with her sister.

"I… I am just…" Revati struggled to bring it up.

"You haven't come out with a book since almost a year. Your mother-in-law told me that you had started working on a book – a thriller for a change."

"Yes, I… I was working on my first thriller because…" Revati was lost in thoughts for a moment, but then continued, "Aarav wanted me to write a thriller. But then he had gone… forever, and I've lost my motivation to write."

"You can always start over," Ruchika said placing her right hand on Revati's left hand.

"I wish to… I hope to…"

"This is a sleepy hill-town with a lot of interesting people. I will take you around, maybe you can find some kind of motivation in them?"

"That would be very kind of you, *akka*."

"But you know, Revati, I would love to see you writing a love story. That is what people love from you… those beautiful sagas about love, those undying stories of love…"

"When my own story of love died away in front of me, I realized that I was only being a hypocrite in my stories. The real world doesn't sustain love; it is just an illusion like the idea of immortality," interrupted Revati.

"As long as you are living, I would love to see you sustain it with those who are still living with you," Ruchika pushed those words harshly on to the shaken heart of her sister.

Revati did not respond. The car swiftly passed on the highway, and suddenly Revati broke into a scream that forced Velu to press down on the brakes. The inertial impact dislodged everyone from their seats.

"Did I run over somebody?" Velu asked sarcastically.

"No... I..." Revati looked around. She realized she was on an empty road, and there was no truck speeding towards them. "I thought I saw... I saw a truck..." realizing that she had experienced another aftershock, she apologized, "I am sorry, I just..."

Kriti who was staring at her aunt, then looked at Ruchika and whispered, "Is Revati Maasi really mad?"

Ruchika put her finger on the lips and gestured to Kriti to keep quiet.

"Daddy said that, not me!" the little girl tried to defend herself.

Ruchika rolled her eyes at her daughter while Kriti made a face and went back to staring at her aunt, who was now looking outside the window as if the world was over. Ruchika knew that things were not going to be easy, she had to bring her sister back to normal with lot of care and love. It was going to be a long season of rain.

A s the car drove through the narrow alley, Revati's eyes opened to a vintage country house that was perhaps built by some colonial colonel of the nineteenth century. A long path of gravel showed the way towards the front door, while the lawn on either sides of the pathway made sure that the grass was green all around. As the dark clouds covered the sun, the car stopped and the writer, enchanted by the haunting beauty of the vintage home, stepped out into the grass. She could not let her eyes sway away from the house. The stone cladded walls reflected class and antiquity while the damp air smelled of moss. She walked around the left side of the house and stood in front of the *Ezhilam Paalai,* or the seven-leaved tree commonly known in the world as the Devil tree. The tree which bore scented white flowers was huge and overlooked the house from the southern side. The branches of the tree were strewn downwards like the hair of a mad woman seeking asylum in the darkest of the rainy nights. It was nothing like the usual devil tree that can be seen elsewhere in the country. It was infamously linked with almost every scary folktale that generated from this part of the country. The sound of thunder gargled in the darkening sky. She could hear the sound of something perching on the branch when something interrupted her gaze.

"You can stare at the tree for as long as you want from your room," said Vishu who had come behind her. He continued, "Come, let us go inside before it starts raining."

She turned around and started walking back towards the car. Noticing that her luggage was being taken by the driver, she went straight towards the front door. Little Kriti was waiting at the door to welcome her aunt. She had plucked and decapitated petals of a bloody red rose flower and threw it in air, as her aunt made her way inside.

"Welcome, Maasi. Welcome to my home sweet home!" the little girl said as the petals fell over her cheeks.

"Why don't you show maasi her room?" Vishu asked his daughter in a mellow tone. He turned to Revati and boastfully mentioned, "I myself got it cleaned up for you dear. It is unused and now looks as good as a new one."

She started walking towards the wooden staircase, "This way Maasi, your room is upstairs."

As the girl started walking, Ruchika turned towards her sister and added, "Settle down, in the meantime, I will make dinner…"

"…No need for that trouble, my lady!" interrupted Vishu, aping the accent and tone of an impaired Italian chef, "Chef Vishu has already got everything ready for his dearest ladies." He winked at his wife.

"My God… I hope my sister has a strong digestive system in place!" Ruchika commented sarcastically.

A tiny little speck of what looked like a smile appeared on

Revati's face. Then she followed her niece and ascended the staircase. With every step that she took, she could hear the heels of her footwear tapping on the moist wood. The sound so produced was sending a reverberating echo which pinched in the deepest corners of the auditory neuron in her brain. The little girl walked across the corridor which led inside a room that had been cleaned very recently.

"This is the room that I wanted but Dad would never let me have it. Now that you will be here, I will be coming here more often," Kriti exclaimed her joy in the most innocent manner possible. She swirled around in circles and popped onto the bed.

Revati ran her eyes across the room. It did not remind her of the apartment where she lived in Mumbai. This was something different, but something very familiar about it gave her nostalgic impulses. The room had an entrance door, a door that led to the bathroom and a window right across the door, and outside the window stood the eerie Devil tree. There was a teakwood bed, an oak table near the window and a cupboard in the corner. She heard the same perching sound, and noticed a crow on the window's sill. Revati walked towards the window and was about to shoo away the depressing black bird, when Velu came inside the room with the luggage.

"Ayyo! No madam. Please do not drive away crows. They are the departed souls of our loved ones."

"Uff! Velu uncle, you are so superstitious!" Kriti stated as she sat up on the bed, "You will find lot of crows here, ugly black ones that go *kaw kaw kaw...*" the little girl imitated the sound made by the crows.

Revati did not react. She just kept looking at the crow. Velu dropped the luggage on the floor. The sound of impact drove away the crow. This brought a laughter on little Kriti's face. Velu could not hide embarrassment from his face. After watching the crow disappearing into the dark branches of the Devil tree, Revati turned around and spoke, "Thank you, Velu. Your words shall not be forgotten."

"Thank you, madam!" he said and moved out of the room.

Revati turned and looked towards the dark branches of the Devil tree. Amidst the darkness, she noticed a reddened eye of the crow. The very next moment, a lightning bolt struck the Devil tree sending Revati swivelling back in shock. The eye was not to be seen, and the window pane came down and shut itself. She turned towards the bed to realize that the little girl had left. Suddenly the writer felt claustrophobic.

"Maasi? Aren't you coming down for dinner?" came the little girl's voice from the door.

Revati turned around towards the door. The struggling writer pulled herself together and answered, "I will be there after a bath."

The little girl left, and with her leaving, the very feeling of loneliness resurfaced and loomed over the writer's mind. She had come here to escape the demons of the recent past, but somehow she did not get a good feeling about it.

Revati kneeled down near her bag and unzipped it. She pulled out some of her clothes and towel. The snow-globe laid in one of the compartments. She took and placed it on the table near the window. After taking her things, Revati zipped the bag and carried the bag and her suitcase towards the cupboard.

"Revati!" the voice of Ruchika came from downstairs.

Revati closed the cupboard's door after keeping the luggage inside and quickly went to take a bath.

The table was set for an extravagant dinner. Ruchika and Kriti took their respective seats. Velu had brought the white ceramic plates and laying them on the dining table. Revati came down the stairs and entered the dining room. Kriti patted the chair adjacent to hers and invited her aunt to sit there.

"Maasi, you are looking so refreshing in this color," the little girl admired looking at the green colored salwar that Revati had worn after taking a shower.

"Thank you dear." The writer smiled.

"Don't be too surprised if you see Vishu sporting an Italian *mooch*," Ruchika joked.

The very next moment, Vishu showed up in an Italian chef's costume, "Madame, presenting Exotic Paneer Salsa with Masala Fusili for my vegetarian wife," he said placing a bowl of the mouth-watering delicacy, "And authentic Manglorean Fish Biryani for my not so vegetarian princess," he said placing a bowl of biryani in front of his daughter.

Kriti took in the aroma of the biryani, "Mmm… Dad, smells awesome!"

Ruchika removed the lid from her bowl, picked up a fork from her table and plunged into the bowl and ate a piece of the paneer. She remarked, "It is okay!"

The grin on Vishu's face comically turned into a frown as he twitched his eye, "What would you know about authentic Italian taste, huh!"

He turned towards his sister-in-law and pulled out that grin over his face again. He restarted his commentary, "And for you, my sweet mademoiselle…"

"You do understand that mademoiselle is French, don't you?" Ruchika reminded him.

"Bloody local people, why did I ever marry this tasteless woman?" Vishu said ignoring his wife's taunts and continued, "Guess what the world famous chef Vishu has prepared for his beautiful sister-in-law… presenting…"

Velu came from the kitchen with a casserole and placed it in front of Revati.

"Chapatti," the driver turned butler said innocently.

"Idiot!" Vishu clenched his teeth, "that is tortilla!" He looked at Velu angrily and murmured, "Not chapatti! Bloody country fellows!"

The turn of events made Revati giggle for the first time. Ruchika noticed this and felt relieved for she had been trying to get Revati out of gloom for a quite some time.

"Actually, I like it," Ruchika stated.

"Of course, you do. After all, who made it?" Vishu boasted.

"Dad," the little girl slurped the spice off her thumb and said, "It tastes just like the biryani from Mrs Mary's Restaurant."

Velu started coughing as if someone had just blown their cover. Vishu lowered his eye brows and gestured to Velu to shut up.

"Wait a minute!" Ruchika picked up a piece of pasta from the plate and smelled it, "Of course, that's why it tastes so familiar and perfect!"

"What are you saying?" Vishu asked as he served Revati some spring onion curry.

"Why does it taste like Mrs Mary's restaurant's food, Dad?"

"Velu had bought the spices and ingredients, ask him!" Vishu tried to dodge the bullet and pass the buck to his helper.

As everyone looked at Velu, the handyman started tip-toeing towards the kitchen, "I think I forgot something in the kitchen."

"Yes... yes, even I forgot something in the kitchen." Vishu escaped with a shameless grin on his face.

"Excuse me... waiter!" Ruchika called her husband back, "What have you bought for dessert from Mrs Mary's hotel?"

"Mmm... ice cream pudding?" Vishu replied in an embarrassed tone.

Vishu and Velu came back from the kitchen with some bowls of ice cream pudding and placed them on the table for the ladies. Little Kriti couldn't wait to have the ice creams.

"Do not even think of eating too much ice cream, young lady," Ruchika warned her daughter.

"But Mumma, there is only one scoop," Kriti alleged.

"That's more than enough. No sugar overdose!" Ruchika turned towards her sister and asked, "How is your Mexican chapatti?"

"It is very good, though it has a Malayalee touch. I like it," Revati commented as she finished the last piece of tortilla on her plate. She ventured towards the ice cream pudding.

"Good, so do not forget to tip the waiters for bringing such delicious food from the restaurant, and pretending as if it were prepared by them," Ruchika said looking at her husband.

"Okay fine, I give up!" Vishu said exasperated as he removed the chef's hat and slammed it on the table, "I did not make the dinner!"

Revati started laughing at Vishu which brought a smile on Velu's face. Kriti joined and soon all of them were laughing heartily. Ruchika knew that Revati made the right decision by coming to stay. Ruchika had complete faith in her husband and daughter with whose help she'd bring her sister back to normal. There were people who awaited the return of Revati Krishna – The Queen of Romance.

The clouds in the sky draped over the dimly lit moon as the atmosphere flashed with lightening. It was one of those nights; horror writers would gloriously describe in their ghost stories. As everyone in the house slept at the hour of midnight, Revati kept tossing and turning in her new bed. She was unaccustomed to the place and the room. She was restless in her sleep as if she was having a nightmare. The light of the partly visible moon crept in through the glass window that was closed for the wind was blowing outside. As the moonlight glowed on the writer's face, a dark shadow of a crow intruded the scene. The intruder fluttered its wings and watched over the writer as she woke up from her sleep. Revati looked towards the window from her bed, but there was not a single being to be seen, just the moon peeping from the clouds. Suddenly, a lightning bolt flashed outside. Revati felt cold and she wanted another blanket over hers. Hoping to find the blanket inside the cupboard, Revati got up from the bed and walked towards the corner where the cupboard stood.

The writer pressed on the knob of the cupboard but it appeared to be jammed. She pressed harder again. The pressure was enough to open it. Inside she saw her briefcase and bags stacked neatly in the compartment. There were some bedsheets and blankets as well. While pulling out a blanket, Revati's eyes fell on something that was kept under the blanket. It was an old typewriter. A classic Smith Premier model of 1905. Vintage stuff lying in the cupboard that had some old government department's label sticking on the surface. Revati curiously pulled out the typewriter and placed it on the table. But before she could type anything, the couple inside the snow-globe moved in a rhythmic manner. Revati attention went toward the snowglobe, but it had not moved at all. She thought that she must have imagined it. She looked at the little couple inside the globe. They reminded her of their wedding day. She felt a presence in the room, she looked towards the window. There was no one, but the shadow of the branch of the Devil tree. She was sure that she had heard a sound, but then she realized that it was coming from the door.

Revati turned and looked towards the door and what she saw surprised her.

"Maasi?" Little Kriti called out as she stood at the door to Revati's room.

"Kriti, what happened dear?" Revati asked as she kept the snow globe on the table.

"I do not like thunder and lightning. Is it okay if I sleep here tonight?"

Revati looked outside and realized how frightening it must be for a young child, especially in a secluded place like theirs. She got up and walked back to the bed. She raised the blanket and gestured the little girl to get inside.

"Did you have any nightmares?" Revati asked.

"I do not know, but I felt like there was someone outside my window," the little girl opined innocently.

The very next moment, lightning struck the Devil tree outside, shocking the hell out of Revati. Little Kriti jumped onto the bed and clung to her aunt. The two of them looked towards the window.

"Maasi, will you promise me something?"

"Yes, dear?"

"Please do not tell mom that I slept here. She doesn't like girls who are afraid, she will scold me," Kriti pleaded.

"Oh dear, do not worry. We will tell her that you were talking with me and fell asleep while listening to my story. How does that sound?" Revati offered, trying to put up a smile on her face against the backdrop of a terrific stormy night.

"Promise?"

"Promise!" Revati added, "And you know what? Your mom never slept alone. She always had me keep company. Did you know that?"

"Really?"

"Yes. I think you are a brave girl already," the writer consoled the little girl although she felt guilty of shaming her own sister by lying about her.

Kriti smiled, and then her eyes fell on the snow globe. She gently took it in her hands and shook it, sending the little white snow particles in an entropic chaos. While looking at the little couple, she asked, "Maasi, have you ever wished that Aarav uncle comes back?"

The rain gushing outside was witness to the state of mind that the writer had been when she heard the little girl ask such a penetratingly painful question about her deceased husband. She could not reply with a realistic no, but then she did not want to think about the impossible either. Sighing in her breath, she said, "Sleep dear child, sleep. Maasi is very tired. Good night!"

"Good night, Maasi!" The girl wished back.

Revati could feel the burn mark left inside her heart. The painful void that was created by the man she loved. She wished, from the bottom of her heart, that Aarav would come back again. As she looked towards the window, she saw a glimpse of her dead husband's silhouette. As another bolt of thunder flashed outside, she realized it was just the cloth stand. She pretended that it did not matter, and just like the little girl, she closed her eyes.

And then the shadow of the intruder appeared; this time over Revati's face.

The morning rays of the sun fell intensely on Revati's face. The rain from the previous night had left a brilliant rainbow for the pleasure of the early riser. Little sparrows tweeted on the branches of the Devil tree as though they were bemused at the drops of rainwater clinging to the bark of the tree. Revati woke to the sound of her cellular phone ringing. She realized that she missed a call from her publisher and the filmmaker who had been after her for a romantic thriller, and that it was nine in the morning. Her sleep pattern had changed for the worse. Little Kriti had already left the bed, perhaps hours ago. Revati got up from her bed and went downstairs.

The kitchen was a war zone for the family. Ruchika was busy making breakfast for herself, Vishu and Kriti. Kriti was trying her best to bunk school by feigning a stomach ache, and throwing tantrums to support her cause.

"Mom, I am having a terrible stomach ache, I swear!" Little Kriti tried to bargain.

"Of course! Who asked you to finish the ice cream last night?" Ruchika accused her daughter of stealing the ice cream from the fridge after dinner. She opened the refrigerator, pulled out an empty brick pack of strawberry ice cream and placed it on the table in front of the little girl.

The little girl looked at it embarrassingly, but kept her ground, "But Mom, I did not eat your ice cream. I didn't even know that it was there in the fridge," the little girl's eyes moved towards the left where she saw her father entering the room while fixing the knot on his tie. She pointed towards Vishu and alleged, "Dad must have eaten it!"

"I did not, young lady." Without removing his eyes from the knot, he went to Ruchika and asked, "Can you just help me with this… important client meeting today."

Ruchika nodded her head in dismay and spoke as she started working on her husband's tie, "I am just tired of you guys. When will you give me peace?" She fastened the knot of the tie.

"Look, I don't have time for all this," Vishu started walking out of the room, "We will talk about this when I get back. Bye!"

Revati entered the kitchen as Vishu stormed out of the house. She sat on the dining table next to Kriti. She smiled at the little girl but in reply she got a finger on the lips.

"Hi Revati, hope you had a good night's sleep." Ruchika changed her tone from *I will kill you* to *everything is perfectly normal*.

"You haven't changed a bit, Didi!" Revati smiled at her sister, "you are still as tense in the mornings as you used to be when I was in school."

"I guess I will always remain the super tense mother my entire life," Ruchika replied as she poured coffee in a tumbler and placed it on the table in front of Revati.

"Thanks Di. But what is the big issue of the day?"

"See this?" Ruchika pointed towards the empty box of strawberry ice cream and stated, "There was almost half a kilo of ice cream in that pack last night. This morning I get up and open the fridge, there is nothing left."

Kriti gently dipped her head as if hiding from another round of allegations. Ruchika looked at her daughter and then continued, "How can they be so shameless? They steal ice cream from the fridge at night!"

"Who?"

"One of them; Vishu or Kriti."

"It could also be Revati Maasi!" Kriti passed the buck.

Revati gave a stern look to the little girl. The girl cracked into a cute grin. When the writer looked back at her sister, she noticed that Ruchika was staring at her in a suspicious manner. "What? Am I in the list of suspects too?" Revati asked.

"Gosh! I will go mad!" Ruchika shrugged her shoulder, "Kriti, go upstairs and get dressed," she instructed her little girl.

Kriti got up from her seat and started to leave.

Ruchika then turned to Revati and "You should also freshen up, have breakfast and then we will leave."

"Leave? Were we supposed to go somewhere?" Revati asked.

"We are going to the school. I thought it would be great if you come along. We are having a seminar for all the parents, and many of the students and parents are your fans. And I think they must have been informed that their favorite writer is coming, so, they must be expecting you," Ruchika mentioned the last few words slyly.

"Didi, why? I came here to find solace, and you are trying to push me to meet people? And that too without seeking my permission first."

"Dr Lakshmi had asked me to make you interact and mingle with people."

"Come na, Maasi," Kriti peeped into the room and pleaded, "At least, I won't be stuck with Hitler in the car!"

Revati broke into a smile at the little girl's comment. Noticing the smile on the writer's face, Kriti jumped in joy and ran to her room to get dressed for the seminar at her school. Ruchika knew that the presence of her daughter and husband was helping Revati come back to normal. She desperately wanted Revati to start writing again. Hours ago Revati's publisher, Jayantakumar Bose, had called on her phone to check whether Revati was alright as she had not answered his call sometime earlier. Ruchika had promised Bose that she would get Revati to start writing again. Ruchika knew that the only thing which could bring back Revati to normal was her passion, and the love of her fans which she would see when she would meet her readers at the school.

The sun had been shining brightly since the morning. An aged white Ambassador car was puffing smoke out of its exhaust pipe as it tried to whimper through the narrow road that led to St Augustine's Convent School. The road was exceptionally congested because of the seminar at the school. Worried at the way they were slowing down in the traffic, Ruchika had her heart pounding at the edge of her ribs.

"What took you so long, Velu? I had told you that we have a session with Sebastian at nine in the morning. I particularly told you to come before eight o'clock," Ruchika inquired.

"Madam, there was a police checking while I was coming. When the police let me go, a black cat crossed my path," Velu replied.

"So?" Ruchika asked surprised at the excuse.

"So, I waited on the road until another vehicle came and crossed the path."

"What?"

"If a cat crosses your path, then you should never pass it. Bad luck! Even death!" Velu said rolling his eyes as he looked at both the ladies sitting in the backseat.

Revati nodded her head.

"Velu uncle, you are so superstitious!" alleged Kriti who had been sitting in the front seat.

"We are late, as always. But I don't want Revati's image to be tarnished on her first visit itself," Ruchika stated her grief.

"Madam, don't worry. I know a shortcut," the driver offered with a big grin. He added confidently, "We will reach the school in just ten minutes."

"Are you sure, we will reach in ten minutes?" Ruchika asked doubtfully.

"Yes, yes! I took that shortcut yesterday to drop Kriti baby at school," he said looking at the little girl sitting on the seat next to him.

Ruchika looked at Kriti. The little girl nodded, then turned ahead and started holding on to her laughter.

"Okay, let us take the shortcut," Ruchika gave her approval.

Ruchika and Revati looked at each other before Revati turned her face towards the window, and started gazing at the world outside. Velu took a sudden turn and they were on an untarred road that passed through the forest. Revati felt a different vibe altogether and she looked up and noticed birds, mostly sparrows and ravens, fluttering in a chaotic manner.

"Were you able to write something in the night?" Ruchika asked bringing Revati out of her gaze.

"Uh… well, not really. I am still trying to figure out if I should start a fresh novel. I don't feel like continuing what I was writing earlier. It just… reminds me of…" Revati stopped at the very thought of Aarav.

"What were you writing about?" Ruchika tried to know.

"Well, I was…"

Before she could finish, suddenly the car jerked and Ruchika's head hit the ceiling of the car.

"My God, Velu!" Ruchika shouted.

"I am sorry ma'am. Just for a short while the road will be like this. We will be out of here in five minutes, then it is just walking distance to the school," Velu responded.

The twelve-year-old vehicle moved on rocky gravel and the bumpy road went on for a stretch before the car finally stopped after five minutes on that path. Velu got out of the car and ducked down before he got up and came inside the car.

"There is a small problem," Velu stated.

"Is there? I thought you stopped to pay the toll," Ruchika responded sarcastically.

"Ha ha… come on madam. There is no toll here in the middle of the jungle," Velu replied innocently without understanding neither the sarcasm nor the frustration behind her sarcasm.

"What happened, Velu?" Ruchika asked while trying to hold on to her nerve.

"Flat tyre! The front tyre has got a puncture," Velu replied in a serious tone.

"Uff! There must be the spare in the trunk of the car."

Kriti could not wait or control her laughter anymore. The little girl finally opened her mouth, "We are using the spare tyre, Mom!"

"Yes, the tyre got punctured yesterday as well, when I took this route." Velu looked towards the sky, scratched his beard like Sherlock and suspected foul play, "There is something strange about this path. I am telling you, it must be haunted."

"The path is not haunted, idiot! The path is not meant for

vehicles to be ridden on," Ruchika exploded at the driver's negligence.

"How far is the school from here?" Revati asked Kriti.

"Just five minutes on foot," the little girl replied.

"I believe we can walk to her school. Velu can get this fixed and come later to pick us up," the writer stated her plan. She had already opened the door of the car.

"Fine. Did you hear that, Velu?" Ruchika asked.

"Yes madam. I will fix this and come. You guys can go."

The two women and the little girl got out of the car and started walking towards the school. Incidentally, they could see the grand cross of Jesus towering over the chapel beyond the coniferous trees. Revati felt fascinated by the place and the magnetism pulled her to think that she had been here in the past. As they walked, someone was watching over them. Someone was watching Revati, and then it flew away, with its black wings masquerading in the darkness of the jungle.

St Augustine's Convent School

The assembly ground was empty as the trio of Revati, Ruchika and Kriti marched towards the school's entrance. There were few parents here and there as they sped towards the indoor auditorium. Joy, one of the peons, saw Ruchika. He rushed to her and said, "Kids are to be sent to their classrooms, parents at the auditorium. Let me take Kriti to her class, you can go to the auditorium. Father Joseph is disappointed with your late arrival."

The three could hear someone talking on the microphone. Joy took Kriti's hand and they started walking to her class.

"Oh God, Sebastian has already started the session," Ruchika said slapping the palm of her right hand on her forehead, "Father Joseph is going to fire me this time for being late."

"What is this session about?" Revati inquired.

"The police department has tied up with an android app called 'Nirbhay', and they have come to give a demonstration. The app will be made compulsory for all kids in the school,"

Ruchika explained.

"You mean that these kids are allowed to use mobile phones in the classrooms?"

'They are allowed to carry mobile phones to school which they have to keep in their lockers. They get them back while leaving the school premises."

Revati nodded her head suggesting that she understood the rules of the modern-day school.

They entered the auditorium in the middle of the session, just before the demonstration began. Everyone's attention went towards the women who entered so late. Few of them recognized the face of the bestselling writer. It was embarrassing for Ruchika as she noticed Father Joseph, the man in white, tapping on the surface of his wrist watch. Ruchika made a sorry face and merged into the crowd.

On the stage, a well-built stout police officer was already halfway into the presentation, speaking in his baritone, "Moving on…" he took a breather and then continued, "Elders have always imparted this lesson to kids regardless of their gender – Never talk to strangers. But how many of us actually listen to that? Do parents these days impart this to their kids? Do you?" he posed the question, "Unfortunately, more and more kids are falling prey to various anti-social elements because of negligence. Not just kids, women are equally vulnerable. Kidnapping, rape, violence, chain-snatching. You read about it in the newspapers every day. Other than putting the blame on the police and the state, what can you do about it? What can an individual do if she is stuck in such a situation, and there is no police or for that matter, anyone around?" Inspector Sebastian looked at the faces of the eager parents. As expected, he saw fear and confusion on the faces of most of them. He looked at Revati, as if he recognized her and smiled.

"This App is the solution," he displayed his phone to the audience, "How does it work? Well, I will invite the Queen of Romance herself to the stage to demonstrate this app for all of you," he said as he smiled at Revati.

Revati was taken by surprise because she was never informed about such a thing. Everyone turned and looked at her eagerly. She started walking to the stage in a reluctant fashion.

When she got up on the stage, Sebastian came close to her and asked, "May I have your phone, please?"

Revati unlocked her mobile phone and handed it over to the inspector with a slight hesitation.

"I am sure that Miss Revati Krishna needs no introduction, right folks?" he asked looking at the people, "She's our favorite writer." He took the phone, opened the app market and downloaded an app. He continued his instructions on the microphone as he proceeded, "I have downloaded Nirbhay from the app store and as you can see, it is an app with a red coloured icon. When I press, it opens this. You will be asked to save three numbers – one each from family, friends and the police. I have entered my number in the police section, now would you mind entering the number of two of your closest people in the other two sections, please make sure that they are present in the crowd, so that everyone can see the demonstration," he said handing over the phone to its owner.

Revati typed in two numbers.

"Now, save it and close the app. It will keep running in the background," Inspector Sebastian added, "Imagine that you are alone and stuck with a stranger who is trying to snatch your necklace or money. What can you do?"

"I believe, I will use this app, of course," Revati replied.

"But how? A thief would snatch your phone or even shoot you if he sees you dialling a number on the phone."

"I don't know, please enlighten us."

"I would request you to quick tap on the screen of your phone thrice with any two fingers in a rhythmic pattern," the policeman instructed.

Revati did as Sebastian said, and the very next moment his phone started beeping. Sebastian was getting a call from Revati, and two more phones in the crowd had started to ring – they were those of Ruchika and Father Joseph.

"This was an SOS call made through the app to the three saved numbers. It will also alert them through a series of five SMSs. The app will also start a voice recorder for safety purposes. Ladies and Gentlemen, we understand that it is the duty of the police to provide security and maintain law and order in the country. But sometimes, we cannot be everywhere, therefore, we strongly insist each and every person to use this app for themselves. The installation of the app has been made mandatory for all kids coming to this school, as a security measure because a child was recently kidnapped in the nearby town. This is a simple step for the safety of our loved ones and it will also help us serve you better," he said and then turned towards the writer and thanked her by shaking her hand and showing her the way down the stage.

Everyone in the crowd lauded in applause.

Father Joseph turned around and started walking towards the exit door. He saw Ruchika on the way, standing in front of him, a little embarrassed.

"Good morning, Father!" she greeted.

"You can wish me good morning tomorrow, it is afternoon now," he said tapping the surface of his wrist watch.

"I am so sorry. Our car's tyre got punctured on the way," she reasoned.

"Of course, that is exactly what your daughter told me yesterday when she was late. Have you trained everyone at your home to lie?"

"No, Father! Honestly, it is Velu who takes us through those bad shortcuts."

"Plans of the diligent lead to success, as shortcuts lead to misery," Father Joseph quoted from the *Book of Proverbs*. "He who follows the path of the Lord doesn't take shortcuts, the devil does."

Ruchika did not really know how to respond because every time the pastor referred to the Bible, she drew a blank over her face.

"My sister, Revati, is here," Ruchika tried to change the subject.

"Yes, I noticed. Why don't you bring her to the office? We can talk there," Father Joseph instructed passively as he glanced towards the stage where he could see the parents and Inspector Sebastian meeting and greeting their favorite writer.

Inspector Sebastian could not stop blushing as he next stood to Revati, holding his phone out to click a selfie with the bestselling writer.

"My wife is a huge fan of your writings," the man in khaki informed after clicking the selfie. He continued, "She even has those collectible box set of your books."

Revati smiled.

"Please, you should come to our home for dinner or lunch. My wife would be delighted to host you," he invited her.

"Of course, I will," Revati replied humbly.

Revati noticed that Ruchika was gesturing to her to come as her elder sister left the room with Father Joseph. Revati excused herself from the Inspector and the spectators, and walked out of the auditorium.

Moments Later
Principal's Office

"How do you feel about our little town?" asked Father Joseph as he sipped the coffee from his mug.

"I… It is a calm and quiet place," Revati stammered.

"The soul of the countryside seeps inside the city dwellers heart, one cell at a time. The charm of the city shall subside and make way for the calm of the countryside sooner or later," the pastor stated as he would do in his sermons.

Revati wove a half-lit smile on her face. Ruchika prayed for the session to be fruitful as the two sisters sat in the room filled with numerous awards and shields won by the school over the years. Father Joseph was proud of the achievements of his students and would never leave any chance to include anecdotes of his achievers in his sermons. The room was well ventilated and the lone window allowed ample light of the sun to come inside and embrace the residents of the room.

'Few days ago, Ruchika told me that you were coming to stay here for a while. In fact," he looked at Ruchika and continued, "your over protective sister here wanted to resign from her job, so that she could be with you at all times."

Revati did not know about this, and she turned her face and eyed her sister in disbelief.

"Loneliness can be very demeaning. That's why…" Ruchika tried to explain but she was interrupted by Father Joseph.

"I could possibly not let another teacher leave us when we are just three months away from final exams. So, I came up with an alternate arrangement that should resolve many problems at one go."

"Mrs Mary, our English teacher for classes eleventh and twelfth had to undergo a major surgery in between the semester. She is on bed rest for the next four months. When Ruchika told me about you, I saw a solution to the school's problem, a solution to Ruchika's dilemma and your personal trauma. The school needs a temporary English teacher, and who else could be better than a renowned writer in the language itself?" He gave a statutory pause and then continued, "Ruchika wanted to be around you at all times, what more can she ask for when the two of you can be in the same compound during school hours?" He looked at Ruchika and then concluded in a consoling tone, "And lastly, my dear child, you have to get out of that trauma, and what better way to keep yourself engaged than with the company of positive young souls who look up to you as their inspiration?"

"Wait!" Revati stated anxiously, "I have never done this before."

"You have addressed so many crowds on so many occasions. This is going to be just like that," Ruchika said trying to convince her sister into taking up the offer.

"Didi, I am not sure if I am even ready for something like this," the writer added adamantly.

"Revati, we all have to go through the pain of separation in life at one time or the other, that's the way God works. But it is always part of His Divine Plan." He placed the mug of coffee on the table and continued, "Here, you won't feel alone, you will always have people around you. Our students will give you the best time of your life. You can also write in the library during free time."

Father Joseph paused and waited for Revati's reaction. He was hoping for some kind of a positive change in her body language.

"It is very kind of you, Father Joseph. However, I don't think I am ready to face the world like I used to," Revati said and sighed.

Joseph looked beyond Revati, at the picture of Jesus Christ hanging on the wall across the room. He spoke prophetically while looking at the picture, "We are not forcing you to take this decision, but I think it will be good for you. I have seen people recover from the gravest of mental conditions just by keeping themselves engaged. And rightfully so, because the human mind is very weak at this stage, and it is vulnerable. If you do not keep it engaged, then it will attract evil."

Just then the crow appeared and sat on the window sill. Revati who was following the pastor's words, got distracted by the appearance of the intruder. The soulless eyes of the crow stared at the beautiful writer. She was physically present in the room but her mind had drowned in that stare of the intruder. The words of the pastor was not audible anymore as all she could hear was the fluttering of the crow's wings.

"Are you with us, Revati?" Father Joseph asked patting on the writer's left hand's wrist that was rested on the table.

"I am sorry." Her eyes moved towards the Father and her sister, "It was the…" she looked towards the window again only to be left startled for there was no crow at the window. Confused, she silenced herself, "Never mind."

"God gives you choices. Make the right choice, it will be your gift," the pastor spoke with clearer intentions. "Take the wrong one, it is your curse. Your choice can benefit hundreds of children for the rest of their lives. The choice I give you starts at nine in the morning tomorrow." He lifted the mug in his left hand and concluded, "I am sure that you will make the right choice."

Revati nodded silently. She did not look very determined but the final words of the pastor did move the humanitarian in her. The chance to impart knowledge to students had paved way into her heart, and she was thinking about it all the time after she had left that principal's rusty room till the moment she was back in the damp room of her sister's house. With less than twelve hours to go, she had to take a chance, make a choice. What would she choose? And more importantly, would her choice affect the events in that sleepy town? Only time would tell.

11 p.m.
Colonel Cottage

The sisters sat on the couch all curled up and cozy. Ruchika's wedding album was wide open and right above the mammoth sized album was a smaller album that had *Goa 2010* printed on top. Ruchika flipped the page and a picture of the sisters running out of a pub opened up in front of them.

"Is this the…?" Revati tried to know the obvious.

"Indeed, our night out in Goa before my wedding," Ruchika said clearing her sister's doubt. She had that smile of accomplishment on her face.

"That was something I would never do again. Never ever ever…" Revati rolled her eyes as she tried not to remember what they did that night.

"Oh come on! It was fun. Going to a cheap bar, dressed up like drug peddlers and getting drunk."

Revati pulled the blanket over her legs and alleged, "Yes, and then we got chased by desperate customers who were not only trying to buy drugs that we didn't have, but were also hitting on us as if we were…"

"Really? Did that happen? I don't remember that." Ruchika scratched her head.

"Of course, you won't," Revati sighed and continued, "Because you had passed out drunk. I had to drag you down to the cab on my shoulder and then put you to bed in the hotel. Do you know how much tension you gave me that night?"

"Revati, for once you had to be my mother." Ruchika smiled.

Revati realized that indeed that was true and it was nothing compared to all these years as Ruchika stood by her like a rock solid figure. Revati felt like hugging her elder sister but the ego within her didn't really allow her to. Ruchika who knew that came forward and held her sister in embrace.

Revati looked at her sister and said, "Yes, you had always been my mother."

When Ruchika flipped the page, a picture that had come out of some other album fell out. Revati picked it up from the floor. It was a picture from Kriti's fifth birthday. The moment her eyes fell on the photograph, a haze of gloom and grief covered the sparkle in them. Tears filled up and started streaming down her face. Noticing the sudden change in mood, Ruchika took the picture away from her sister.

"Do not go back to that state of mind. He is not…"

"I know that he is not coming back," Revati interrupted Ruchika. She wiped the tears from her face and said while getting up, "But sometimes… I just wished that I could see him one more time, you know," Revati sulked, "Just to see his face is all I beg for… just once because that moment when that truck hit us, I didn't see his face. All I remember seeing was that truck coming towards us. I wanted to see his face, if I had to die. But *your God* was not kind enough. Neither could I see him, nor did he let me die."

Ruchika looked at her sister helplessly. She felt mentally weak as she could not produce words competent enough to calm down the emotionally driven writer who got up and started leaving for her room.

11:30 p.m.

Revati entered her room and shut the door. She walked to the table near the window where she had kept the snow globe and the typewriter. The moonlight fell on the glass surface of snow-globe and penetrated into the sparkling snow particles that decorated the little couple inside with the gilt and glamor of romance.

With tears in her eyes Revati wished, "Why can't all this be a nightmare? Why can't you come back?" she said and was about to turn around when the writer's instinct made her want to use the typewriter. She went back to the cupboard and found some A4 sized sheets lying inside. She quickly got back to the table and inserted the paper into the carriage of the typewriter. This was an older model that used a moving carriage which consisted of a cylindrical platen, paper table, paper bail and some other parts.

Revati did not have a chair to sit. So, she turned the table towards her bed, so that she could sit on her bed and type. After setting the margins, Revati gently pressed on the letter 'T'. The carriage moved to the left as she typed. She finished typing the title of her new book when a thunder struck outside near the devil tree. This was followed by a power outage. It wasn't unusual in that part of the country especially in that weather. The electricity department would cut off the power supply during thunderstorms in order to avoid electrocution. As the lights went off, she could not see anything on the keyboard. Unlike her laptop which had a keyboard with backlit display which helped type in dark or light. She decided to call it a night and went to the bed.

As the writer pulled the blanket over her and closed her eyes, the intruder arrived at the window. The shadow of the crow formed a distorted projection on her lovely face that sang a melancholic strain of the past.

12:46 a.m.
Revati's room

It was just amazing, the very feeling of holding hands of Aarav and dancing to a wedding waltz in her bridal dress. She had the most amazing feeling when it started snowing. It was as if the snow globe became real. Or was she trapped inside that snow globe… Forever? Suddenly, the feeling of claustrophobia started gulping her from all sides as a thick patch of blackness covered her from all directions… And then a demonic figure popped up wearing a reddish orange mask.

She woke up on her bed, panting for breath. She was sweating in the cold weather and her heart was pounding like the chef's hand that kneads the dough. She switched on the light, but it would not work. She got up and started walking towards the window for she saw a sight which scared her. The snow globe was not where it was seen before she slept. It had fallen down. Just then the branch of the Devil tree bristled in the wind outside. She closed the window and noticed the reflection of her face on the surface of the window. Something about it attracted her to walk closer towards the window. She stared at her own face's reflection as if she had never seen her face before. The branches danced to heavy wind and the sound of it could not be heard inside the room. And then suddenly, the face on the window changed to someone else's. In a flash of a second, she saw someone else on the window, someone as beautiful as her but younger... much younger. She recoiled in shock. As she tried to catch hold of her breath she noticed someone standing near the tree on the ground. Before she could look at it, she was distracted by a series of nervous knocks on the front door.

Revati thought that it must be Kriti, just like the previous night. She must have felt scared to sleep alone. Revati looked back at the ground from the window but she saw nobody there. She turned and walked towards the door. She lit the torch on her mobile phone and opened the door, but there was nobody outside the room. She wondered if Kriti had knocked and gone back to her room. She decided to check on Kriti and started walking towards her room. She opened the door to her little niece's room only to find her sleeping at peace. She closed the door and started walking back when she heard it again – nervous knocks on the door... the front door.

Revati came down the stairs. She felt as if a long spell of drowsy piano tunes rolled in her auditory lobe. Just when she reached the door, the phone's battery died and the source of light went off. In the darkness, she pulled the latch and opened the door but the door could not cross the safety chain. Before she could remove the safety chain, a girl's hand came in through the gap formed between the door's edge and the door's wooden frame. Revati fell back and screamed in shock.

Woken up by the scream of her sister, Ruchika jumped out of her bed and came running to the front room where she found Revati lying down on the floor gasping for breath. Vishu followed Ruchika.

"What happened? What are you doing here?" Ruchika asked anxiously.

"I… I… I saw someone outside," Revati said pointing towards the ajar door. She continued describing in a despaired state of mind, "Her hand… it was all covered with… bloody hands…"

Vishu went towards the door and opened it by removing the safety chain. He looked around for a moment before coming inside.

"There is no one outside, Revati. You must have had a dream," Vishu said as he closed the door.

Ruchika helped Revati get up and as she got up she noticed a blood trail that went towards the door.

"There… look!" Revati exclaimed pulling Ruchika by the arm, "Blood marks, I told you."

Ruchika noticed that there indeed were some blood spots on the floor. However, she remembered the fact that Revati was having her dates. She kept calm and helped Revati back to her room. She gestured to Vishu that she would take care of the situation.

"Revati, you had a bad dream, that's all. Let us go back and put you to sleep again. We have a big day tomorrow, and for a change, let me take you to school on time." Ruchika forced a smile on her face to console her sister.

Revati looked bewildered as she walked up the stairs to her room with Ruchika. As the sisters went inside the room, there was the little niece who was watching everything as it happened. Ever since Revati arrived at their house, Kriti had started feeling that there was something weird about her aunt. For her young and innocent mind, scientific terminologies and psychiatric explanations did not make much sense. She was seeking explanation in the unknown.

St Augustine's Convent School

The students of class eleventh's C section were known to be the most notorious ones in the history of the convent school. Father Joseph had tried left, right and center to bring order to the chaotic class. Despite terminating the rogues, the class still continued to be as undisciplined as before, as if the devils had passed on their traits to the remaining students. The class knew pretty well that Joseph would not suspend all of them as it would bring a very bad reputation to his school. The principal was very careful about the school's reputation. The principal pushed open the door and allowed Revati to enter first. The principal of the school and the interim English teacher were standing in the class which was engaged in early morning gossip, fist fights on the teacher's table and of course a group of young wannabe pilots were testing their paper planes by throwing it out of the window.

Father Joseph raised his eyebrows and then made a gurgling sound with his throat. This quickly caught the attention of the class and everyone looked straight at the new entrant. Pin drop silence followed.

"Aren't you supposed to do something when someone enters the class?" the pastor asked.

The students looked at each other. Some of them looked at Revati with disbelief, while few girls had an excited look on their faces; definitely readers of the Queen of Romance.

Nodding his head, the father instructed, "Stand up and wish your new English teacher!"

The students got up in unison and after a moment sang together, "Happy Birthday to you…"

'Shut up! What are you doing?" the furious principal fumed at the students.

"Father, you only asked us to wish her, but never told what to wish, so we assumed it was her birthday and we wished her following your order," said Muthu, the boy who was the leader of all things notorious in the class.

Father Joseph picked up a piece of chalk lying on the floor and threw it at the dark skinned boy. Everyone laughed.

"Now wish her good morning, idiots!" Father Joseph ordered.

"Good morning Miss!" the class said in chorus.

"Good morning everyone." Revati smiled.

"This is Miss Revati Krishna. I know that many of you are already very excited about having the most popular writer of India teach you till the end of the term." Father Joseph glanced at Revati and said, "I am sure that you will give her memorable time here at St Augustine's… and maybe inspire her to write a book about her time here, with all of us as her book's characters." He stepped back as he paved the way for Revati to take over. He went towards the door and exited.

Revati walked to the teacher's table and sat on top of the table. She looked at the entire class from right to left. Some of the students were eagerly waiting for the writer to speak, while there were few who were not very pleased, but there was one particular person who only seemed to be present in the class physically. It was clear from their faces that they were looking at a writer for the first time in their life.

"All of you know my name, and I am assuming that some of you have even read my books," she said looking at the girl on the second bench of the third row who was smiling continuously. Revati asked, "I would like to know your names, please."

The students started introducing themselves.

"Rahul Raj."

"Anthony P."

"Emil Selvaraj."

"Prithviraj Sukumaran." Some students started giggling at hearing the name that was similar to the name of one of the most popular Malayalam superstars.

"Suriya Sivakumar."

"Devi Menon."

"Fathima Ali."

"Lavanya Ravichandran," mentioned the girl who was smiling earlier.

"Beautiful name!" Revati stopped to compliment.

"Yes, ma'am. It was the name of the heroine of your first book. My favorite!"

"Thank you, dear. I have request to the entire class. Please do not address me as ma'am or miss. You can all call me by my name – Revati."

The students were a little confused because they were never used to calling their teachers by name, at least not in front of them. Father Joseph was very particular about addressing teachers as ma'am or sir.

"I believe that respect is something that comes from a person's heart. It need not come if the mouth forcefully says sir or ma'am." Revati cleared the doubts of students, "Alright?"

"Yes, Revati!" the class replied in chorus.

"Good, so... next!"

The boy sitting in behind Lavanya got up and said, "Yaqub Ali."

"Yaqub Ali?" Revati asked as if she misheard the name.

"Who Yaqub Ali?" the boy asked confused.

"You just said that your name was Yaqub Ali," the writer opined.

"No, ma'am..."

"... Revati!" the writer reminded.

"Sorry, Revati. I never said Yaqub. My name is Muthu."

"Are you playing some kind of a prank with me, Muthu?" Revati asked with a raised eyebrow.

"No, not yet," Muthu replied.

"Revati... he never said Yaqub. He said Muthu," Lavanya interfered in support of the boy.

"Okay, Muthu what?" Revati asked for the boy's last name.

"Only Muthu. Nothing after that," the boy stated adamantly.

"Muthu never had any parents. Does that make him an orphan or a bastard?" someone murmured from the back.

An enraged Muthu jumped out of his bench and moved across to the last row and pulled out a boy by his shirt's collar and threw him on the floor.

"I am going to make your son a bastard," Muthu claimed and punched on the boy's right eye.

The boy held Muthu by the groin and slapped on his face. The fight just got real and it was something that Revati had never witnessed in her life. She tried to stop the fighting boys, but apparently a group of kids were already enjoying the brawl. Revati went out of the classroom, helplessly looked around and found the peon.

"Can you please call Father Joseph!" Revati pleaded.

The peon rushed to the principal's office and brought him to the classroom where Revati was standing like a damsel in distress, not knowing how to control the boys who were now bleeding. Father Joseph came inside the classroom and pulled Muthu by the ear and dragged him to the principal's room.

Revati stood there inside that class in a breathless state terrified by the scene she just witnessed. It may not have been as tragic as the one she witnessed right before the truck came and hit their car few months ago, but it was disturbing enough. She wondered if she could survive that place at all.

Few minutes later
Abandoned Washroom, Ground Floor

She opened the tap and let the stream of water fall on her
hand. Revati splashed it on her face. She looked at herself
in the mirror and all she could notice was the reflection of the
dampened wall behind her. The toilet smelled as if it had never
been cleaned in years. She would have thrown up if it wasn't for
her mind that was preoccupied by the intense battle that broke
out in her classroom on her first day as a teacher.

Another splash and then rested her hands on the wash basin,
and looked at herself in the mirror. Her face had started showing
wrinkles, she had never noticed that before. Aarav would always
joke about her getting wrinkles much before him as she was older
than him by age. She wished that Aarav was alive and nothing of
this sort would have happened; she would have been in Gurgaon
writing her books, playing mommy to a beautiful little girl or a
boy. That was the plan in life which was now shattered into a
gloomy wrinkled face that stared back at her from the mirror.

And then suddenly, right behind Revati's reflection, the girl appeared on the mirror. The same girl who appeared on the window the previous night. This time, Revati could see blood coming from her eyes; like tears It rolled down her face that was tattered and bruised. The face with sharp features was haunting to look at, especially with the rope-marks on her neck. Revati jolted in horror and her hand hit the bottom of the washbasin, sending down a piece of the old ceramic on the floor. As it broke into pieces, she heard a clinking sound. The girl in the mirror was gone and Revati only saw a distressed reflection of herself in it.

She inhaled and exhaled slowly. She stepped on something metallic. She noticed that there was a rusted key on the floor that was probably hidden inside the wash basin's ceramic neck. She picked it up and observed it in the light that came through the small ventilator that opened to the woods on the backside of the school. The rusted key was hardly two inches in length but was of sturdy quality. Despite being old, it did not bend at all. It had something carved on it. There was not enough light, so she took out her mobile phone and used the screen's light to read what was carved on it.

Revati's eyes popped out of their sockets, for what she saw was exactly what she had heard few moments ago.

With a needle or a compass, someone had engraved a name on it:

Yaqub Ali

4.45 p.m.
Senior Staffroom

The senior faculty staff room was deserted as everyone except Ruchika and Revati had left. Ruchika was packing her stuff. Revati sat next to Ruchika. Only those teachers who were in charge of the extra-curricular activities in the school were all busy in preparations. Christine, the Tamil teacher, came in gasping and slammed the interschool fest's brochure on the table. She kept the bag hanging on her shoulder above the magazine and started searching inside it. She took a breath and then turned towards Revati who seemed to be lost in a confused state of passive thinking.

"Wow! I cannot believe that I am actually in the same room as you, Revati Krishna. It is an honour." She pulled out a copy of *U Me Forever* from her bag and gave it to Revati, "I have been keeping this in my bag ever since I heard from Ruchika that you were coming to teach in our school. Would you please sign this for me and my son?"

Revati took the book from the excited Tamil teacher and signed it for her.

"Thank you so much," she said as she received the signed book from its author.

"You are welcome... uh..." Revati waited for her name.

"That's Christine Selvan, our school's very own Tamil teacher," Ruchika introduced as she finished packing her stuff.

"Ruchika, how is your preparation for the fest?" Christine asked.

"You know how they are. You tell them left, they go right!" Ruchika commented sarcastically at the dysfunctional troop she was handling, "I am sure that we are proudly going to retain our championship in Carnatic music this year as well."

"Championship?" Christine appeared confused, "But your troop never won any competition in the history of interschool fests."

"Exactly, my troop will be crowned champions from the bottom, just like last year and the year before when we will finish last," Ruchika forecasted.

Christine laughed at Ruchika's comment.

"Besides the Malayalam Declamation and Debate, I have heard that we have some great chances to win in the Malayalam Poetry and Sanskrit Recitation category this year," the Tamil teacher passed on the rumour.

"Really?" Ruchika asked in disbelief, "Malayalam, I can understand. But since when did Father Joseph start sending participants for Sanskrit recitation?"

"Well, he didn't. But one of our students is apparently interested and she signed up on her own."

"Well, that's rebellion. Hope she wins!" Ruchika winked at Christine.

"She is really good, I have heard her chant the quotes from the Gita, and she just mesmerizes." Christine lowered her tone and whispered, "and she is Muslim!"

Revati was one of those people who could not stand such typecasting of people on the basis of religion or caste. She sighed at the narrow-mindedness of the teachers even if it included her own sister.

"What is wrong if a Muslim girl chants a *shloka* in Sanskrit or a Brahmin boy recites an *aayat* from Quran?" the writer snapped at the Tamil teacher immediately.

"Nothing. I just…"

Before the question turned into a series of heated exchanges, Kriti entered the staffroom with her school bag and water bottle. She ran to her aunt and hugged her tightly, "Maasi, how was your day?"

"It was alright, dear," Revati replied as the little girl's warm embrace calmed her mood.

"Yes, and what you saw was absolutely normal at 11th C, by the way," Ruchika remarked jokingly, "Muthu only broke his nail this time."

"What do you mean by *only*?" Revati asked.

"Well, last month, the boy broke his toe and fractured another one's jaw," Christine revealed.

Ruchika laughed at the incident and said, "Welcome to St Augustine's!"

'Hey Ruchika, All of us have to stay back at school till eight in the night from day after tomorrow till the end of the school fest," Christine informed her.

"Is it? God! Thanks for telling me. I must inform that idiot Velu right away. Last time I did not tell him and the buffoon took Vishu to Cochin, and I kept waiting here till eleven in the night."

"Mom,' Kriti asked in a tone filled with utmost curiosity, "When you were stuck here that night, did you meet any ghosts?"

"No! There are no such things as ghosts," Ruchika dismissed.

"I have heard my friends say that there is a ghost who comes after midnight. It comes in the abandoned toilet in the ground floor," the little girl said in an eerie manner.

Revati's ears stood up as she realized that she was there in that toilet earlier when she saw the haunting image of the beautiful girl. Little did she know that it was an abandoned toilet.

"Abandoned?" asked Revati.

"Yes, nobody goes there anymore. It has some drainage issues," Christine unveiled the mystery. "Anyway, I must take your leave now. I will see you tomorrow. Goodbye!" said the Tamil teacher and started to leave with her bag.

Christine had forgotten to take the fest magazine with her and it lay there on the table. Revati curiously picked up the magazine to see what was the fest all about. She flipped the pages one by one, studying each and every competition that was to take place in two weeks from then. What she did not realize was that even Ruchika was standing at the door, prepared to leave with Kriti.

"Are you planning to stay here for the night?" Ruchika asked as she stood at the door, ready to leave.

"Come Maasi, let us go now." Kriti pulled her aunt's left hand.

The magazine dropped from Revati's hand and it fell with its front cover down on the floor. Had she seen the picture on the back cover, it would have sent a chill down the writer's spine. But she did not, for the little girl pulled her aunt out of the staffroom which was empty thereafter for the day.

On the floor, the magazine laid. And on its cover was the picture of a masked man, the red paint glowing disproportionately on the man's diabolical face.

12:46 a.m.
Revati's room

The clouds had started covering up the moon once again and a thunderstorm was raging in the distance. However, the rain gods had decided to play spoilsport to an otherwise perfectly dry wintry December. Now the days were dark and the nights were home to thunder and bright lightning bolts.

Revati hadn't slept yet. Although the wind blew harshly outside, the room was cosily warm because Revati had closed the window. She had decided that she would write at least one chapter a day. However, the whole day had passed but she had not been able to write anything. The paper on the typewriter was blank and staring at her bluntly. She started typing something but stopped and hit backspace to clear the written words. Alas, the poor typewriter's backspace did not work as expected. Frustration led her to bang her fist on the bed where she was sitting.

Revati decided to switch back to her laptop as the typewriter's obsolete modes weren't doing her any favour.

With the laptop on battery mode, the writer continued staring at the monitor blankly when suddenly the gruesome image of the girl appeared again. This time on the screen. She immediately shut the lid of the laptop in shock.

In the darkness, she could only see when the thunders flashed outside. Revati closed her laptop and tried to meditate as advised by her doctor. She felt like something was coming towards her, but she didn't open her eyes and tried to focus on her breath. But suddenly she started feeling colder. Thus, the writer opened her eyes, she saw the window which was open.

Who opened it? She thought as the window had not been opened since last night and she remembered that she did not even go near it. She got up and tiptoed towards the window but on the way she felt like heard knocking from behind. This was just like the sound she had heard the previous night.

Who could it be? Is it the girl? I am sure I am not imagining all this, she told herself.

The perturbed writer made an about turn and went to the door. Like the previous night, there was nobody outside her door, but then she heard it again, coming from downstairs.

As she reached the front door, she heard heavy breathing from the other side of the door.

"Please help me…" said a young girl's voice.

Revati immediately opened the door, but once again there was no one. She used the mobile phone's torch to look around. She noticed fresh footprints on the muddy soil in the front yard. Revati closed the door and followed the trail that led her to the empty road on the eastern side of the cottage.

She walked further on the road until she entered the woods. She didn't know if she should continue when she heard the cawing sound of the crow. The writer's ensnaring eyes watched the intruder who was staring at her in a hypnotizing gaze. It started flapping its wings and then glided down towards the chest of the writer. Revati felt frozen, she could not move and the crow touched down and passed into the writer's paralyzed body and there appeared a flash of light. Revati could not understand what just happened but then she saw someone running into the woods, it was a girl… the girl. Or maybe it was just another hallucination.

Another flash of light appeared in front of her eyes, and she felt like nothing had changed. Intrigued by the visual, Revati walked into the woods. She took the same path as the girl. As she walked through the path between towering trees, she could hear the whispering of a young man and the giggling of a girl. But she could not see anyone or anything but trees, grasses, moss and the light of the moon peeping through the leaves and the occasional lightning flashes.

She reached to that point from where she could see a lake flowing beyond the woods. Something crashed behind the trunk of tree to her left. Revati walked around and noticed that there was a boy, hardly of eighteen, struggling in pain.

"Pa… P…" he struggled to speak as he rested his back against the tree's trunk.

Revati looked at the boy in a clueless manner.

"Parvati…" he said finally looking into the writer's eyes, "run for your life!"

Revati was surprised, "Parvati? You must be mistaken…"

"Run!" he screamed at the top his voice, "Don't worry about me."

"Who are you?" Revati asked.

There was no reply, and her eyes blinked. When she opened her eyes, there was no boy either. However, she noticed something clinging on the branch coming out of the trunk. It was a necklace with a locket that could be opened. Something was engraved on the backside of the locket but she could not read it.

She opened the locket and saw a picture of the girl inside, the girl who had been haunting her ever since she had arrived at the place.

It started raining, and the drops of icy rain fell on her body. She gazed into the girl's face in the locket.

Parvati, run for your life! The boy had said. *Why did the boy say that? Was Parvati the name of the girl in the picture? What was she warned to run away from? Was there someone after her life?*

As Revati's mind started churning out theories and speculations, she heard wet footsteps approaching from behind amidst the sound of rain drops touching the ground. Someone was coming, for sure.

Was that the one from whom the girl was supposed to run away from? Revati thought. She did not want to turn around as fear had started seizing her mind, but the curiosity of the writer proposed to think the other way. A twig cracked on the ground, under the foot of that someone. With a rock placed on her heart, she turned around.

The writer screamed again, as the feeling of claustrophobia ironically cornered her in the open space as she saw the terrorizing masked man charging towards her. The red color of his skin seemed like it was painted with the blood of his victim.

His pointed canines gleamed under the light of the moon. This wasn't a man at all. It was the devil himself.

The devil pushed Revati on the wet ground. The accumulated rain water started flowing into her ears, and she could feel a reverberating deafness echoing inside. The devil pounced on her like a lion preying on a timid deer.

"I am not going to let you go tonight, bitch!" the devil hissed in his shrill voice.

Revati struggled and hit the devil on his face with her right hand. She could see that the red paint of his face had got stuck on the palm of her right hand. He arrested her by grabbing both her hands and then kneeling over them. He brought his face closer to Revati's face, and sniffed her lustfuly like a wolf.

"I have waited for long…" He locked his eyes with hers and pronounced, "Parvati Subramaniam…"

The name brought images in the writer's mind that was taken over by horror. A bolt of lightning struck the tree behind her and that flash of thunder forced her to close her eyes.

When she opened she saw a man on top of her. However, it wasn't the man with the red mask. This was the face of a man she knew well. It was Vishu – her brother-in-law. She couldn't believe her eyes. She looked at her hand, but the red paint was also gone.

Few minutes later
Inside Colonel's Cottage

Revati was bruised and her wounds were bleeding. She was sitting on the couch with a pillow placed on her back.

"What were you doing in the woods?" a concerned Ruchika asked.

"I am glad that I found her before she was eaten by some wild animal," Vishu interrupted as he brought first aid with him. He unzipped the bag and took out the cotton wool and betadine solution to clean Revati's wounds.

"I think I should put a lock on your door so that you do not go outside in the night," Ruchika exploded as she saw her sister writhe in pain when the betadine solution touched her wound, "You did the same thing last night as well, though you didn't go out like tonight."

"Didi, I swear by the gods that you worship," the writer who had lost her faith paused and said, "I saw a girl, I heard her voice," Revati produced in her defence.

"You are imagining it. Dr Lakshmi had mentioned…"

"No, this was not like that. There was someone else too. A young boy…" Revati recollected and added, "and a…"

Vishu interrupted Revati, "When I came there, I saw you struggling and fighting against yourself. There was no one!" He started walking towards his room, "It would be good if you just go to sleep. I have to leave for Bangalore early in the morning. Revati, it would go good if you can see Dr Lakshmi on Skype or something. Let not this thing eat up your head."

As Vishu went inside his room, the sisters sat there on the couch. Ruchika could understand that her husband had had a long day and he had been trying to get a business deal sealed for almost a month. She forgave him for his insensitivity towards her sister. She finished winding the bandage on Revati's arm.

"That was the last of it. Are there any other cuts?" she asked Revati.

"No. But the one inside my heart shall never heal." The writer replied in her usual metaphoric manner. She sighed and then remembered something, "Didi… do you know anyone called Parvati…" she tried to recollect the full name, "Parvati Subramaniam?"

Ruchika thought hard, but she could not place that name anywhere. She said, "No, I can't remember. Why?"

"Just… I think I need to rest." Revati decided not to think about the matter.

"Yes, that would be the best thing to do now. Do you want me to give you company in the room?" Ruchika offered with concern.

"No, I will be fine. Thank you, Didi," Revati replied and got up from the couch. Upon noticing that Ruchika was about to walk her to the bedroom, the writer requested, "Please, don't worry. I can walk to my room."

"I will see you in the morning, goodnight!"

"Goodnight!"

Revati ascended the staircase and walked into her room. She had witnessed something horrific moments ago. She was sure that it was a hallucination as nothing sane could explain those visions. Even if it did, then she would be facing a plethora of questions that would need answers. Perhaps someone was already waiting for the answers, or maybe someone was waiting *with the answers...*

But who was she?

Parvati Subramaniam.

9:30 a.m.
XI-C, St Augustine's Convent School

The classroom was unusually quiet that morning. Revati had finished her lecture on E.V Lucas's famous short story, *The Face on the Wall*. Revati remembered it as one of the most intriguing stories that she had ever read while in school. She had asked the students to write a brief report on the story about a man struck by influenza who sees the face of a stranger on the wall of his room. She sat on her seat and looked towards the window as the class silently wrote the report in their notebooks. The emptiness of her heart fulfilled the visuals of the vacant playground outside the window. The gentle breeze was flowing into the room, and it looked less cloudy than the previous night. The wound on her arm from the previous night's struggle in the jungle seemed less distracting than the lifeless view from the window.

The weather is so unpredictable, just like people, she thought and turned ahead to check if her students were at work or not. Some of the backbenchers were holding on to their tendency to chatter during lectures. She felt nice that the students were in more control than they had been on her first day. She wondered if Father Joseph had given them some punishment the previous day. She was about to get back to staring thanklessly at the window when she took note of one of the girls in the middle row resting her head down on the desk. Revati got off her seat and went towards the girl's desk.

"Dear, are you alright?" said Revati as she tried to wake the girl up by softly touching her shoulder, but the girl did not move an inch. She was stiff as dead. The writer turned teacher pressed on the girl's collar, and tried to get her up.

The girl got up suddenly, and to Revati's shock, it was the same girl's ghostly face- Parvati Subramaniam. This time however, the face was cut and blood was dripping from her cut wounds, and there were scars left by thorns on a face that was covered with dirt and mud.

"Pa... Parvati?" Revati screamed and ran to the door.

"Revati!" the girl called.

Revati looked back at the girl, but it was not a monster anymore. It was her fan, Lavanya, who was equally shocked at the turn of events.

"What happened? Why did you run?" Lavanya asked.

"Why were you sleeping in the class?" Revati asked in between shivers.

"What? I was never sleeping. You came to me and then stood in front of me, staring at me like a statue." The student recollected in disbelief, "And who is Parvati?"

Revati did not have any answer because her mind was asking the very same question – *who is Parvati?* The writer looked at the class, and from Muthu to Lavanya; it felt like everyone was staring at her with judgmental eyes. She waddled her way out of the class as she could not take it anymore.

Revati bumped into Father Joseph in the corridor while he was on his round. He noticed the paleness on the writer's peach-like face.

"What happened? You look as if you just saw a ghost!" said Father Joseph as if he had the power to read minds.

"I… I am not feeling well," she replied.

"Did you hallucinate again?" he asked.

"Hallucinate? What do you mean?"

"Well, Ruchika told me that you have been hallucinating about something ever since you arrived here," Joseph revealed.

"I am telling you that what I saw last night was not a hallucination. Yes, it was not there in front of me, but it was there at some other time," Revati claimed.

"My dear child, the mind plays games when you are weak from the inside. The more you think about the past, the weaker you will become."

Revati realized that there was no point in defending her stance and proving it to a man who has always been used to imposing his beliefs onto others. She sighed.

"Father, can I… Is it okay if I go home?" Revati requested.

The pastor saw the tears building up in her eyes, but being the strong woman that she was, they did not allow themselves to trickle down her face.

"I will ask someone to drop you in my car," the kind pastor offered and said, "I will tell Ruchika about it. You don't bother, and go home, get some rest."

11 a.m.
Principal's room, St Augustine's Convent School

After sending off Revati, Father Joseph had sent the peon to summon Ruchika to the principal's room at 11:05 a.m. Knowing Joseph's stern adherence to punctuality, Ruchika made sure that she was sitting in his office right before the allotted time. The door opened and Father Joseph entered the room.

"What a surprise, the great Ruchika is on time!" the holy man remarked as he passed her and sat on his chair.

'What happened, Father, is everything alright?' Ruchika inquired as she glanced at her wristwatch. She had a music class commencing in ten minutes.

"It is about your sister."

The look on Ruchika's face changed, "What about her, Father?"

"She had another one of those hallucinations today in class," the pastor revealed in a very grave tone.

Ruchika slapped her forehead, "Oh god! Not again. Last night she was assaulting herself in the woods."

"Woods?"

"Yes, the one that encloses Kurmallur river. My husband found her."

"Dear Lord Jesus, why would she go there? Don't you people lock your houses at night?" Joseph asked angrily, "That poor child, you know there are foxes and leopards in that area."

"Vishu had locked the door in front of me, and then we went to bed," Ruchika paused and then stated her disbelief, "I am still wondering how did she open the door when it was locked and the only key remains under my husband's pillow."

"I would suggest you to take her to a psychiatrist for a second opinion."

"I told her the very same thing this morning but she refused. She believes that the incidents were not hallucinations," Ruchika surrendered.

"Yes, so she told me too."

"You know I have been trying to know something from people around here, but everyone acts weirdly when I ask them about her."

"About whom?"

"A girl... Revati keeps repeating that she saw a girl."

"A girl?" Joseph crunched forward on his chair.

"Yes, do you happen to know any girl by the name..." she paused to take a breath and then pronounced the two words constituting her full name, "Parvati Subramaniam..."

Father Joseph's eyes widened in a state of disbelief. The weather had started changing outside, it was getting cloudier... darker.

11:06 a.m.
Revati's bedroom, Colonel Cottage

It was dead silent inside the house, and Revati felt like having come to a cemetery in some dystopian world. She kept her bag and glasses on the table next to her bed. She looked at the snow globe that was lying on the bed. She placed it back on the window sill again.

The thick dark clouds rubbed against each other emitting bolts of lightning. The bees and birds rushed to their nests, while there was one being that seemed to enjoy the incoming evil. It was the intruder. The crow sat well protected on a crooked branch of the Devil tree. The aphrodisiac smell of the devil tree's flower loomed poignantly in the air.

Inside, the unsuspecting writer was getting ready to take a bath in the tub. Revati undressed and draped a bathrobe on her naked body. She walked into the bathroom and filled the tub with hot water.

She dropped the robe and stepped into the warm water of the bathtub.

The intruder was watching her.

11:08 a.m.
Principal's room, St. Augustine's

As the dark clouds parted to allow drops of rain to touch down the earth, Father Joseph emerged from his locker room with a dusty folder that was at least a dozen years old. He kept the folder on the table and then opened it carefully after he sat down.

"No one at St. Augustine's would want to talk about her," the father revealed and gestured to Ruchika to check the file.

Ruchika pulled the folder towards her and started flipping through its clipped pages.

Sixteen-year-old found dead in Kurmallur Lake

The newspaper clipping was taken from the local newspaper and pasted on the piece of paper. She flipped to the next page which also contained a newspaper cutting.

Attempt to Rape or Rape? Kurmallur Mystery Continues

"The journalists as usual made sure that the case was episodically revealed in the newspapers. It was more sensational that way," Father Joseph recollected in disgust.

The folder contained many pictures as well. There was the picture of a girl who looked like a princess from a Malayalee folktale. If falling in love was a capital offence then the sharp features of her face made sure that any man who looked at her would happily allow himself to be beheaded in prosecution for the crime. She looked so full of life in the picture from her class's group photo that Ruchika almost felt like she was alive and would come out of the picture.

"Parvati Subramaniam…" Father Joseph said.

"Did she…?" Ruchika wanted to know more about the mysterious girl.

Joseph turned few pages and arrived at a crucial one.

Kurmallur Murder– Imam's son convicted for Rape and Murder

The next headline confused Ruchika.

Yakub Ali is the Kurmallur Killer

"Is this…" Ruchika asked, "the same Yakub Ali who…"

"Yes, the very same Yakub Ali whose prosecution has been delayed by a good thirteen years. He did his way with the poor girl and threw her dead body into the lake. The religious politics in this country has let him live so long." He momentarily paused as if he was about to break into a sermon which he did. He quoted from the Corinthians, "For we must all appear before the judgement seat of God, so that each of us may receive what is due us for the things done while in the body; whether good… or evil."

Ruchika was least interested in the pastor's biblical expertise. She was worried about her sister.

"So, this Parvati Subramaniam actually exists…' she corrected herself, "… I mean, existed?" Ruchika asked.

"Yes!" answered the pastor.

"And she died… I am sorry. She was raped and murdered in the woods and thrown into the Kurmallur lake?" Ruchika asked raising her left eyebrow.

The father nodded in agreement.

Ruchika got up from her seat.

"I am sorry, Father, but I must go home."

Ruchika dashed out of the room as she made a call to Velu on her phone.

11:11 a.m.
Revati's Bathroom, Colonel Cottage

Inside the bathroom, Revati felt at peace, as the warm molecules of the water gently caressed the peach like soft skin of her body. She had forgotten to indulge in herself after the death of her husband. She remembered being in the tub like that over a year ago with Aarav. She could still feel his presence. She feared missing the sensation of warmth when his body touched hers in the tub. Revati started feeling dizzy, so she closed her eyes.

However, she was feeling the same as she closed her eyes. She could see him entering the tub, and when she opened her eyes, she saw him right there in front of her... half immersed in the water.

"Revati... it has been so long," said Aarav, his voice pulsated radially as if coming from a time warp.

She did not know if it was her imagination shaping in the form of another hallucination or if it was the ghost of her dead husband. But she did not care. She was too tired to care about the truth.

"Aarav… I missed you so much," she said with tears in her eyes.

"I have come to take you with me. Hold my hand…" he said and offered his right hand.

Like a hypnotized machine, the writer held the dead man's hand. Revati looked at Aarav's cold hands. And before she could know, a red colour appeared on the skin over his finger and started spreading on his body. In shock she looked up. In place of Aarav she saw a man with red skin and a devilish looking red mask. He had long steel nails with which he attacked her and sent her into the water. She drowned under the surface of the water, however when she looked down she realized that there was no bottom.

It was not her bathtub any longer, she was in a bottomless water body. She was drowning in Kurmallur lake. She could only see the red hand strangling her and keeping her head under the water. She could not feel her breath anymore; she was struggling in a losing battle. The red paint in the area of the hand that was under the water was going away and revealing his original skin. She saw something… perhaps it was a ray of light… Whiteness.

For we must all appear before the judgement seat of God, so that each of us may receive what is due us for the things done while in the body; whether good or evil…

Whiteness.

It was completely white and then there were images of Aarav fading in and out as if playing on a slideshow. Then the images faded into whiteness and the whiteness dissolved into blackness.

Her eyes twitched and opened for the first time in twenty-four hours. The bright lights of the hospital room invaded the darkness that had preceded. It appeared as if someone had placed a layer of butter paper in front of her as everything appeared blurry. She could make out from the patterns that something like a door just opened and two people had come inside. One was wearing a white coat therefore, it might be a doctor and the other was wearing a *salwar kameez* that reminded her of Ruchika. Revati closed her eyes. She could only hear the slow beating of her heart.

When she opened her eyes, the things appeared clearer. There was a doctor, quite young and with him was a woman of forty years but wearing a saree that looked quite old fashioned. It was not *salwar kameez* and definitely not Ruchika. The writer flapped her eyelids shut.

When she opened, she saw the same doctor but he seemed to have more grey hair with a thick stubble. She looked at the woman next to him. To Revati's surprise it wasn't a stranger in saree but her sister, Ruchika, in a salwar kameez. The exhausted Revati started breathing heavily. She closed her eyes one more time. She was hallucinating again.

She prayed for Ruchika to be there when she opened her eyes, and then she did. But there was no Ruchika, the doctor was younger and there was the stranger woman in saree. The doctor came near Revati and then slit her throat with a surgical knife. The writer's almost paralysed body roared and shifted on the bed in horror. The doctor held her hand strongly so that she did not move.

"Revati, please. You are safe here," said a comforting voice that belonged to her sister.

The writer stopped writhing and looked around until her eyes fell upon Ruchika. She looked back at the doctor, he was older and had stubble. But he did not have a surgical knife in his hand. Revati realized that she had only imagined all of that.

Another hallucination, perhaps, the doctor thought as he examined Revati's pulse.

"How are you feeling?" the doctor asked the patient as he felt the dropping pulse rate.

"I feel… my stomach feels so light," Revati responded.

"You will be alright soon."

"How long have I been gone?" she asked.

"You have been here for almost a day now." The doctor looked at Ruchika and conveyed. "Your sister brought you and has been here since then."

The nurse came in and handed over the MRI scan reports to the doctor."

"Your brain is fine. Nothing abnormal." The doctor fixed his eyes on Revati and inquired, "Do you get such sessions frequently?"

"No, only since the accident," the writer said.

"Do you have a history of drug abuse? I am just asking because writers take the help of drugs and intoxicants to slip away from reality and come up with interesting creative ideas for their stories."

"No, doctor. I have never done any of those. I write simple stories for ordinary people. I have never needed any intoxicant for writing," the writer stated clearly but in a weak tone.

"Your sister shared your entire medical history while you were unconscious. I saw that you are taking Prozac-22 after the accident, right?"

"Yes."

"Prozac is an anti-depressant that can control anxiety attacks, para-sensory seizures and memory slips in depression patients," the doctor explained, "Do you remember how you got these eel bites?"

"Eel bites?" Revati was confused.

"Yes, the one on your right leg. I understand the strangle marks on your neck as your own doing. But the eel marks on your leg couldn't have been done by you, for sure."

"I don't understand, doctor. I just went for a bath because I was losing my mind."

"Did you go to the lake?"

"No, I went in my tub for the bath. But before I remember, he was there again…"

"He who?"

"The masked man. He strangled me and pushed me into the water, and then I realized that I was not in a tub anymore… it was a lake. I heard him calling me Parvati…"

"…and in the past one week, she has been getting up in the middle of the night and going out into the woods," interrupted a worried Ruchika and continued complaining, "She says that she saw a girl who ran into the woods and a boy who called her Parvati. Yesterday, she saw that girl in the classroom."

"Did you or anyone else in the class see this girl?" The doctor tried to know.

"No," Ruchika replied dismally.

"Hallucinations," he said.

The doctor noted down something in the report and then and walked out of the room. The nurse came and started taking the tests as instructed by Dr Gopal. Ruchika came and sat next to Revati and caressed her forehead. The eyes of the elder sister were filled as she saw the younger one going through such mental torture.

"Do you think that I have finally gone mad, Didi?" Revati asked.

Ruchika gently placed her hand on Revati's and nodded her head in a consoling manner.

Conference room
Palghat Medical Centre

Dr Usha had been waiting in the small conference room of the town's largest medical centre. She was one of the senior most doctors in the region who had an experience of over thirty years in the field. Dr Gopal had already passed on the reports and copies of Revati's medical history to the senior doctors.

"No signs of drug abuse, no records of abuse in history. All blood reports and scans are absolutely normal. A tragic accident, episodes of hallucinations and suicidal tendency," Dr Usha put the file down and removed her spectacles. In a conclusive manner she said, "Psychosis, that's what this is. Isn't it obvious?"

"Yes, that was exactly my diagnosis in the beginning. But I want you to look at these reports as well," Dr Gopal said handing over another set of reports in a plastic folder.

"I hope you remember Parvati Subramaniam."

Dr Usha adjusted her spectacles and looked at the younger doctor as if he had asked a sinful question.

"This is the post mortem report of Parvati Subramaniam. I remember preparing this very clearly because I was the one who had signed on this twelve years ago," recollected the senior doctor. "What has that go to do with Miss…" she looked at the name on the folder, "Mrs Revati Krishna?"

"Dr Usha," the doctor revealed, "Revati Krishna told her sister that during the hallucinations she had heard herself being addressed as Parvati by a nineteen year old boy."

"So? It could be any Parvati… it could Parvati Menon or Jayaram!'

"Yes, of course. But she also went off into the woods, to the lake all by herself, led by her hallucinations. She was found in the woods by her brother-in-law struggling against herself. She said she saw a teenage girl coming at her door and asking for help a night before that incident."

"Lunacy knows no bounds, but have you ever heard of the word coincidence, Dr Gopal?" she asked sternly.

"Coincidence does not explain the mark on her arm and neck," he said and placed two photos of Revati in front of her and then opens a page on Parvati's post mortem report that had pictures of Parvati's dead body with the exact same marks on the arm and neck. He continued explaining, "This was Parvati's body and the pictures in your hand are Revati's which I clicked this morning. The mark on Parvati's neck was made by the rope which was used by Yakub to drown her. *Coincidentally*, there was no rope where Revati was found. And then there are the eel bites!"

"If you jump into a lake, you are prone to get bitten by eels. Kurmallur lake is full of them!" Dr Usha reasoned.

"Except that Revati had drowned in a bathtub in her bathroom."

The senior doctor got silenced by the answer and she sighed. She exchanged glances with Dr Gopal.

"I would have said the exact same thing as you had I not checked these files," explained Dr Gopal.

"Dr Gopal, do you watch the news these days?"

"I am sorry. But what is the relevance of me watching news?"

"Please answer what you are asked."

"Yes, I do."

"What is the most common headline on any news channel, or newspaper or social media feeds?" the senior doctor asked.

"The hanging of Yakub Ali."

"Exactly! And exposure to negative and violent media has serious and long-lasting psychological effects beyond simple feelings of pessimism or disapproval. You are familiar with Dr Davey's theory on the psychological effects of media violence which suggests that violent media exposure can exacerbate or contribute to the development of stress, anxiety, depression and even post-traumatic stress disorder."

"I am." Dr Gopal replied.

"So, I will put it like this…" Dr Usha deduced, "The patient, Mrs Revati, must have read about Parvati's murder after getting intrigued by the media coverage on Yakub. Her brain was already reeling under trauma because of the accident in which not only she lost her baby and husband, she also suffered a head injury. Look…" the senior doctor plucked out a report and threw it towards Dr Gopal. She continued her deduction, "You are a neurosurgeon, base your study on facts. What do you see in that report?"

"Mmm… Head injury and signs of retrograde amnesia, selective in nature," the neurosurgeon read and responded.

"Exactly! She has forgotten few things that have happened at the time of the accident and the selective nature of this forgetfulness has led her to have memory slips. Now, she must have read about this incident and done some research or something when she had the accident. The accident wiped out certain memories including this one. However, the information that the brain had stored started manifesting itself in the form of a disassociated persona."

"Split personality!" Dr Gopal exclaimed.

"Indeed, and she started splitting into a personality called Parvati Subramaniam whom she didn't remember because of the selective nature of retrograde amnesia. She was only doing those things which she knew Parvati had done in the past."

"But how did she know that?"

"She is Vishu's sister-in-law right?" Dr Usha asked.

"Yes."

"She must have heard it from Vishu then. It must have been a casual conversation which she would not recollect due to the memory slip."

"So, you are suggesting that…"

"I am *telling* you that this woman who suffers from amnesia has split into a second personality and in that personality she went to the lake, drowned herself, got bitten by eels. She then somehow came out of it and went back home. Here she came back to her real personality and didn't remember how she got dirty, so decided to take a bath. But she lost her mind in the tub again." The senior doctor rested her case and dropped the report on the conference table.

"I think that would too cruel to say," Dr Gopal said in empathy.

"Dr Gopal, don't be driven by emotions and superstitions. You are a reputed doctor for God's sake! The woman is going through a difficult time. She has been having Prozac that stimulates hallucinations. I would recommend you to stop this medicine. Let's put her under weekly observation first. Let us not link this with Parvati Subramaniam because it will bring unnecessary attention of the media to the patient as well as to this hospital. We must stick to our oath."

She got up from her chair and said, "We are done here, good day Dr Gopal!"

"I had a discussion with a senior doctor." Dr Gopal said.

Ruchika sat in front of him in his room, eagerly waiting to hear his diagnosis about Revati's condition.

"Were you aware of the serious condition that your sister had acquired after the accident?" the neurosurgeon inquired.

"What is it Dr Gopal?" Ruchika asked anxiously.

"Your sister has retrograde amnesia which has catapulted her mind to split."

"She, what?"

"The hallucinations and memory slips are part of that."

'But what about that Parvati? How could she probably know about it?" Ruchika stated her doubt.

"Newspapers or channels?"

"But she has not watched any news channel or read newspapers after the accident. Dr Lakshmi, her therapist, had strictly asked her not to be influenced by the violence and negativity spread by the media," Ruchika mentioned.

"Was Dr Lakshmi the one who prescribed Prozac-22 for depression?" Dr Gopal asked in a slightly aggravated tone.

"Yes, I believe."

"Where did you get the Prozac from?" the curious doctor inquired.

"I think she got it from Dr Lakshmi only. She always has a stock with herself."

"Then, she is not a good doctor. Prozac-22 is banned in India. Did you know that?"

"I… I did not know that."

"Prozac-22 stimulates hallucinations, and it could pull out suppressed memories and deem the brain incapable of distinguishing it from the present's reality."

"What do I do about it, doctor?" helplessly Ruchika asked.

"Instead of Prozac, I will suggest some milder medicines. She can go home tomorrow with you. She will need to perform meditation to focus her mind, and most importantly, it is your love and care that she needs," he said as he wrote down some medicines on the prescription sheet.

"When she was just six years old, we lost our parents. I raised her. If I can do that back when I was just fourteen, then I can surely do a better job now." Ruchika assured.

"Take her out on a picnic or do something recreational. Her mind needs to freshen up. I would like you to bring her in a week's time from now for another check-up," Dr Gopal said.

Ruchika nodded in agreement and got up from the seat. She wondered how she was going to reveal all this to her sister who was at a very vulnerable mental state. She picked up her handbag and started walking towards the door when she stopped and turned towards the doctor.

"Dr Gopal, do you think that my sister is going mad?"

"If I could, I would like to believe in something else... But my rational mind does not allow me to..." he said and smiled.

Ruchika knew that there was something that kept the doctor from coming out frankly about Revati's condition. He did not want to believe in that explanation based on the diagnosis at all. He was clearly asking Ruchika to look beyond the natural...

Ruchika would have to look into the supernatural for an explanation.

Vishu's Tea Estate, Neliyampathy Hills

It was a beautiful afternoon in Neliyampathy hills, one of the most beautiful places in Palghat district of Kerala. The mist of the morning sluggishly hung around as Revati walked in wonderment through Vishu's family-owned tea estate. Little Kriti let go off her aunt's finger and ran into nature's lap. Revati looked at the rural women who were plucking tea leaves and throwing them over their heads into the basket tied to their back. They seemed like automatic robots. However, they stared hard into Revati's eyes. As the writer walked amused by the beauty of nature, she felt as if she had been there before, getting a feeling of *deja-vu*.

"You guys are so lucky!" Revati said to her sister, "You live in such a beautiful place away from the hustle and bustle of the city."

"Of course we are… and it seems like Father Joseph's theory about city dwellers is coming true after all."

"I miss Gurgaon too. No place can ever beat the Millennium city."

"I understand, but you can go back after some time. I know you can't be kept here forever," declared Ruchika.

The sisters walked to the highest point in the estate and stood there looking at the rows of tea plantations in front of them. There was slight movement inside one of the nearby shrubs. Revati and Ruchika did not notice the tremble beneath the leaves and suddenly out of the tea shrubs jumped little Kriti, scaring her aunt and mother.

"Gotcha!" the girl laughed at her mother who almost lost her balance because of the shock.

"You wait… I have told you a hundred times not to jump out of places and scare people." Ruchika tied up her dupatta around her waist and chased her daughter playfully.

The innocent activity of her niece and the bewildered irritation on her sister's face lightened up the mood for the writer. This brought a smile on Revati's face. But there was someone approaching her from the back, and as the distance decreased, Revati started feeling a very weird pull.

"Paru…!" the shrill voice of an old woman called from behind.

Revati turned around and saw an old woman who had tied a woollen scarf over her ears. Hers was a very familiar face. The sight of Revati brought the woman back to her senses.

"I am sor, I thought you were…" she felt embarrassed and she started walking away briskly.

Revati knew she had seen this woman. She had seen this woman in the hospital when she opened her eyes. It was in that hallucination where she had seen a younger form of this woman along with a younger Dr Gopal.

Who was she and why did the woman call me Paru? Revati started thinking.

And suddenly it struck the writer.

Paru… Oh my God! She was about to call me Parvati…

The woman had already gone down the hill. Revati ran after the woman down the steep valley to the foothills where she saw a small hut. Smoke came out of the chimney which was probably the hearth working. It smelled like plain boiled rice was being cooked.

She walked towards the hut. Her heart had started thumping faster than ever but strangely, she could not visualize this place. She did not feel the deja-vu that she felt in Ruchika's house or Kriti's school or even Vishun's tea estate. This place did not remind her of anything, but the woman did. She took a deep breath and then knocked on the door thrice.

And finally the door opened, and in front of the writer stood the same old woman. The same woman in Revati's hallucination when she had opened her eyes in the hospital. Just older than ever…

The woman's eyes started showing signs of tears. Revati looked beyond the woman and right in front of her she could see the wall of small living room where there was a picture. It was the picture of Parvati Subramaniam that stared right back into Revati's eyes.

The interior of the hut was made of brick and mud. It looked like a very simple setup but neither did it look unclean and impoverished. The house was neat but modest in appearance. There were two stools, a red painted mahogany table and a rug on the untiled floor. And of course there was the picture of Parvati hanging on the wall. It felt as if she would come out of the picture and break into her haunting grin. Revati sat on the stool while the old woman brought a cup of black tea and placed it on the table. Revati thanked the woman as she took a sip from the piping hot tea.

"I… I know you, I don't know how. I can't even possibly explain it. But I do. I feel like I have known you since long back," Revati said with a smile briefly lasted on her face. She looked at the picture of Parvati and asked, "Was she your daughter?"

The old woman's eyes filled with tears.

"Yes, that was our daughter. Parvati."

"I am really sorry, but there is something that I want to tell you," Revati cut to the chase without prolonging what she intended to know. "I have been seeing these dreams… rather

I believe that I have been shown these visions by something or someone I cannot explain. I have been called Parvati in those visions… I do not expect any sane person to believe in what I am saying…"

Suddenly the moaning of a sick old man was heard from the small room to the right. Alarmed, the old woman got up from her seat. Revati also felt like she had heard that voice before, she also got up and followed the woman. She went inside the small bedroom which felt as mushy as mould that would grow under a tree in the rain. In the room there was a mattress that was lying on the floor and an old crippled man was spread on it. Revati's hand automatically picked up the glass of water that was kept on the floor and poured the water into his mouth. It was as if she was supposed to do that. Parvati's mother looked at this instinctive reaction of Revati with empathy and surprise.

"He has been like this for the past ten years. We ran out of money due to the case against Yakub, and curing him became impossible… So, we sold off our cottage to Vishu's late father. He was a very nice man. He also gave us this small place to live in his estate," Parvati's mother revealed the intimate details of what happened after her daughter was murdered.

"Wait! You mean the cottage where Vishu lives now was yours few years back?" Revati asked intrigued by this new detail.

"Yes, the cottage with the grand *ezhilam paalai* tree that once used to overlook Parvati's room," the mother revealed as she thought about the beautiful place it used to be once.

The woman continued to speak as Revati had visual flashbacks of the days when Parvati would stand under the tree and look at the ghostly branches wondrously.

"She was attached to that tree. She never allowed anyone to cut it. Maybe that's why it grew so much. Have you ever seen a *paalai* tree as huge as that one?"

Revati did not respond as she was lost in the imageries of a young Parvati looking outside her room from that window where Revati had seen the intruder.

The old woman continued remembering her dead daughter, "Parvati used to spend hours in that room where she would write poems and scribble her thoughts in a journal."

The word suddenly brought Revati out of the visual trance that she had been riding on.

"Journal?" Revati's asked.

"Yes, she was very fond of writing. She had a book of poems and some journals which she would never share with anyone. She used to write them in that typewriter that my husband had brought from office when she was little. After writing, I think she used hide those pages somewhere in the closet room. We could not find it when we left that house. She was very private with her thoughts."

Just then Revati received an sms on her phone from Ruchika. *Whr r u? cm bk. We r leaving. hv to drop Kriti at her friend's place.*

"Thank you Amma, I should leave now. My sister is looking for me."

"Of course, dear. I am glad you came by. It felt nice somehow. Come again soon."

Revati looked at the old man. He had a peaceful smile on his otherwise dead and distressed face. She got up and started leaving.

"For a moment, in the garden, I felt like I heard her," the old woman said as she opened the door for Revati, "I can hear her voice, you know… on windy nights when the thunder bolts the earth, her shrilling voice haunts me."

She stopped to cough and then she bore her eyes and said, "I felt she came back when I saw you. But it was just a feeling. Truth is… the long gone loved ones, they never come back…"

Just as she said that, the crow appeared on the roof of the hut. Revati was quick to notice the intruder's presence.

"Maybe they do… Maybe they do…" Revati said as she looked at the intruder.

10 p.m.
Colonel Cottage

After having a quiet dinner, Revati sat on the couch and switched on the television. The national news channels were holding prime time debates on Yakub and his hanging. She found it funny that a convict was being supported just because of his religious inclination. She felt sad at the fate of Indian politics as she heard some of the topmost politicians of the country defending the undefendable just for the sake of votes. She changed the channel and switched to a local news channel and surprisingly she saw a familiar face on the mini screen. It was an interview of Inspector Sebastian. Revati turned up the volume.

"Inspector, you were one of the policemen in charge of the convict fifteen years ago when the murder had happened. It has been fifteen years and still he has not been punished for the crime of rape and murder. And today, people were protesting to save him. What do you feel about it?" the female reporter asked from the inspector who was at least a foot taller than her.

"I am completely shocked. So many people coming together to protest the hanging of a convict. What is wrong with these people? What would have they done if their sisters or mothers were raped and murdered? Would they have protested then as well? I am very disappointed at the reaction of these so called activists who talk about human rights for rapists, murderers and terrorists," replied the police inspector angrily.

"For now, the court has asked to hang him in three days. Do you think this final appeal to change the decision will work in favor of Yakub?"

"Justice should and will prevail. It will happen in three days," Sebastian replied and then walked away into the police station.

"So, you have finally watched the news!" Ruchika came from behind and said.

Revati felt a little guilty about the fact that she had broken her vow. She had promised Dr Lakshmi that she will not watch any news channel or read any newspaper for a year as part of her therapy. Revati was not interested to watch the program any further, she muted the television. She noticed that Ruchika had a folder in her hand.

"The house seems so darned and silent without Kriti," Revati commented.

"Well, she will be back in a week. She likes staying at her friend Trisha's place. I thought it would be better if she stayed away from all this mania," Ruchika replied.

"I am so sorry for everything," Revati apologized.

"Sorry for what?"

"For putting you through all this trouble."

"Listen, I want to talk with you about this. Let us do that

and then decide if there is any need to apologize or not, okay?" Revati stated her intentions clearly.

Ruchika continued as she looked at the folder in her hand, "I do not believe that all this is just a coincidence, neither do I believe that you are going mad," she pressed on to her sister's hand and assured, "I believe in you. I believe in what you say, but we must find out more about this. Here…" she handed the folder to Revati and told her, "Dr. Gopal gave these to me. Reports of Parvati Subramaniam."

Revati simply took the folder and then kept it aside.

"Didi, I think I know all this already. I don't know how. I can't explain it. It is like someone is telling all this to my mind, you know… like someone is trying to communicate with my mind," Revati explained what was happening to her.

"You mean like the wandering spirit of Parvati?"

"I don't know. I have not seen any ghosts or apparitions," Revati confessed.

"Even if it is true, why would she do it?"

"That's what I am trying to know. The man who brought this fate to her was caught and will be punished for his crime in three days. Then what else would a wandering spirit seek, if it is not justice?"

"What if…" Ruchika locked her eyes into Revati's, "it is not justice?" Ruchika asked suspiciously.

"What do you mean?"

"What if the spirit won't get justice with the hanging of Yakub?"

"You mean, there could be someone else involved?" Revati asked.

Just as they started getting goosebumps all over their body, Vishu entered the room interrupting their conversation.

"I am sorry, but could you women please switch off the light and stop talking. I am trying to sleep but I am not able to. Ruchika, you know that I have to get up early in the morning for my meeting with German Importer." The usually hippie husband vented out on his wife and left cursing.

Revati and Ruchika were surprised. Ruchika had never seen her husband so tense before in her life. She had been married to the man for ten years now. She sighed and got up from the couch. She bid goodnight to her sister and went to her room. Revati was the last to leave. She picked up the folder and switched off the lights. She walked to her room upstairs.

It was going to be a stormy night.

It was a cold night in the hillside town and the rain had taken halt for a couple of days. So, it was obvious to get a cold spot in a previously warm patch. Unlike the previous night, that one was quite silent. Even the crickets and the insects of the night lay dormant in the silence.

In the middle of the night, Revati felt as though someone was around her, and she could see shadows that whispered in quivering voices constantly. The doctor had diagnosed Revati with a split personality disorder that was at the starting stage. The writer refused to digest that and chose to believe in the voices she was hearing. She would never do that otherwise, but now she made such a choice when it happened to her.

She looked at the time on her phone, it was 12:45 in the night. She heard a knock on the door. Unlike the previous couple of times, Revati wasn't terrified or anxious this time. In fact, she was eagerly waiting for the sound for she had started believing that the soul of Parvati did not mean any harm. After all, she was an innocent girl. Revati got off from her bed and went to the door to open it. As usual she did not find anything, but then she heard a sound from the farthest corner of the corridor. She started following the sound that resembled the desperate fluttering of wings. She walked the dark corridor that separated her from the source of the sound.

Yes, the cottage with the grand Ezhilam paalai tree that once used to overlook Parvati's room.

Parvati's mother had told Revati earlier in the day. The words started playing in her head as she started feeling claustrophobic.

She used to spend hours in that room where she would write poems and scribble her thoughts in a journal. Yes, she was very fond of writing.

Revati wondered if Parvati had been alive, would she also have become a famous *writer*. The sounds had started to recede and as she walked further, she reached a dead end. Revati was expecting to find a small room where she could find Parvati's writings. She turned on her mobile phone's light and shone it around but nothing.

Amidst the silence, she heard the cawing sound of the crow, and it came from above. Revati looked up, pointed the light at the ceiling. She noticed a small rope hanging from the wooden ceiling. She made an effort to catch hold of the rope, and when she finally did after couple of attempts, she pulled it down carefully. It was an opening to a compartment in the ceiling. Along with the door, some papers and books that were kept over the wood fell on the floor. Excitedly, Revati picked up the items.

She had a book of poems and some journals which she would never share with anyone. She used to write them in that typewriter that my husband had brought from office when she was little. After writing, I think she used hide those pages somewhere in the closet room. We could not find it when we left that house. She was very private with her thoughts.

"So that's where you hid your writings!" Revati spoke to herself as she pushed close the door to the compartment on the ceiling.

She heard the sound of the crow as if it just said *yes* to Revati's remark.

The writer did not show any patience, she sat on the corner against the wall and using her mobile phone's light, started reading the journals of Parvati Subramaniam. They were all typed on a typewriter.

Indeed, Parvati had a flair for writing and it could be seen in the small paragraphs of thoughts that she had written in what appeared like unstitched journal. There was a set of poetry that had some amazing ballads about love. Most of the them were typed in English, while a few of them were handwritten in Parvati's mother tongue – Malayalam, a language which Revati had long forgotten. Revati had grown up in Delhi and her writings were in English, therefore, she had lost touch of Malayalam long back. However, she patiently read the journal typed in English which had some candid moments from the life of Parvati, as described by the girl herself, which sent Revati down a different lane.

21 March, 2003

Today was the first day of my final year in school. It was a very special day, because he has come back from Hyderabad... after six long years, he is back...

It felt like I had waited for ages, and I was so eager to catch a glimpse of him... and when I finally did, I could only blush, my friends mentioned that my face had turned pink like a rose… And when his eyes fell on me, I knew no bounds of happiness.

He came to me and he asked how I was, and all I could do was turn my face to the other side and shy away… He has not lost his charm at all… he has only gained more… He placed his finger on my chin and then turned it towards him.

More than ever before… he said he loved me…

More than ever before, I love him now…

My Yakukka…

"Yakkuka?" Revati asked herself after reading the entry in the journal. She thought if Yakukka is what Parvati called Yakub. She knew that *ikka* is a respectful word used to address an elder Muslim boy in Malayalam. "Is she calling him Yakukka with respect… or love? She was in love with Yakub!" The bestselling writer wondered and continued to another date in the journal.

2 July 2003,

Yakukka was once again caught in the club house, smoking in the woods with that dirty scoundrel Alfred. I wish… I pray that Yakukka stays away from Alfred… I don't like Alfred at all. Nobody likes him. He is always flirting around with girls. He smokes and drinks in that club house with his dirty friends. Why does Yakukka have to be part of Alfred's dance group? Why can't he listen to me and stay away from Alfred. I feel so uncomfortable when he is around.

"Now who is this Alfred? Does he have anything to do with Parvati's murder?" Revati questioned before diving into the next entry in Parvati's journal.

11 September, 2003

I have topped the half yearly exams… I am so happy… Amma and Appa are excited… Yakukka is busy preparing for the interschool youth fest, and I am busy preparing for my entrance exams… We hardly get time to meet… I am worried because he has started spending more time with Alfred and his group. I hope he does not become like them. I wish I could spend more time with him.

In a few months, I will be appearing for my final exams… after the exams I will start the new life that awaits me… a life with Yakukka…

Revati realized that she had another thing in common with Parvati. Both of them used dots lavishly to depict breaks and expressions in their sentences. By now, Revati had started praying for Yakub and Parvati's love. The romance writer always wanted a happy ending, and so she prayed, even though she knew how it ended.

24 December, 2003

It is six p.m. and after this I will sneak out of my home without informing Appa and Amma because they will not allow me to go to the school for the fest at night. Yakukka will be performing at night and I will get to see him after the performance. This is the night that I have waited for. After two months, Finally, I will get to see Yakukka… I will get him to hold me in his arms.

I am very excited… He has promised something special… A special gift he had said in his last letter to me. A gift that I shall remember forever… A moment of love… after the performance… in the club house…

I feel shy writing this… but the very thought of the moment… gives my heart wings… I feel sad because I will not be taking my dearest typewriter with me. But one day when I come back with my Yakkukka, when my Appa and Amma would forgive me for falling in love with a Muslim… I will take this typewriter back.

I love you Yakukka… I am longing to see you tonight…

It was like someone just cut off a supply of oxygen to a dying patient. That is how Revati felt when she realized that that was the last page to be written in Parvati's journal. Revati switched off the mobile phone's light and then started typing something on the Google browser. She was still sitting on that pathway on the first floor of the house.

Parvati Subramaniam Kurmallur murder

Revati was surprised at first to see that the search query did not return any adequate results. That is when she realized that it is not legal in India to give out the name of a rape victim. So she changed her search query to;

Yakub Ali Kurmallur murder date

And then she got many results. She clicked on the one that was from a prominent newspaper. Her eyes opened wide as she read the date of the murder. She looked at the date of the last entry in Parvati's journal. Both the dates were the same – 24 December 2003.

"Yakub had promised something amazing and called Parvati in the woods. But she was killed that night. Did Yakub call an innocent girl to the jungle and try to take advantage of her by giving fake promises?" Revati asked herself. The blood in her veins had started heating up as she thought about the evil plan that Yakub had devised which cost the innocent girl her life and dreams.

As she started closing the journal a photo fell off from the back cover. It was a group photo of a school fest event. She picked it up and once again switched on the mobile phone's light to see. She saw Parvati, the most beautiful among the girls… and then a young Yakub, whom she had seen in the hallucination. With him were two more boys, one of them was Vishu!

As she started zooming into the photo, she heard footsteps approaching her. She quickly closed everything and hid it in the pocket of her pajama.

'What are you doing here?' asked Vishu who had come in unasked.

"I… I just came here because I heard some sounds," Revati replied as she inched her hands inside the pocket.

"No… I heard sounds," Vishu said sternly, "because you were doing something out here. You, my dear, did not hear any sounds, you imagined them. Didn't you stop taking that medicine?" Vishu inquired in a heartless manner as it seemed that he was no more interested in her sister-in-law's mental traumas.

"I am sorry, Vishu. I will go back to my room. Goodnight!" she said and started walking to her room.

Vishu did not bother to reply. He kept staring at her as she went inside her room. He did not like what was happening in his house anymore.

The students gathered for the morning assembly in the school ground. The ambassador arrived at the front gate of the school. Ruchika got off in a hurry and started running towards the gate. Noticing that her sister did not get off, she stopped and turned around.

"Do you need a special invitation, madam writer?" Ruchika asked in her usual sarcastic tone.

"I will join you later. I have to go somewhere first," she said and waved goodbye to Ruchika.

Ruchika kept staring in disbelief as the car turned and got enveloped inside the thick dark smoke that came out of the exhaust pipe.

Few minutes later, the car had moved out into the highway that connected Palghat with Thrissur. It was another day that was devoid of any rainfall.

"How long will it take us to reach there?" Revati asked Velu as he started drifting off in his usual speed that was way above the speed limits.

"Forty-five minutes, madam," the driver replied as he showed his enormous front teeth.

"That's not a very long drive, is it?" she asked hoping that Velu would not be doing the usual small-talking that drivers do during long journeys. Revati had become a private person after the accident and did not like being bothered especially when her mind was so full of things.

But before she could take a breath of relief, the eager driver asked, "Why do want to go to the city jail?"

"Will you take me only if you I tell you?" Revati asked in a stern tone.

"No madam, I will take you even if you do not tell me," the driver replied innocently as if he did not get affected by the rudeness in the writer's question.

Revati felt bad for coming out so strongly at the driver who had a little child's attitude. She sighed and then apologized, "I am sorry, Velu. I am just not in a mood to talk. There are lot of things running in my head."

"I know, *Vishu Anna* told me," he said smiling as if he had been told a casual incident.

"Vishu anna? You seem pretty close with Vishu," Revati asked as she slowly indulged into small-talks herself.

"Oho, *Anna* and I go back to childhood. My father was the driver here, and *anna's* father was a good man. He became my sponsor and sent me to school with Vishu *anna*. We had a lot of fun in school," he said chuckling at the memories of his school days. "I had always warned him about that girl. She was very treacherous. My *amma* used to tell me that she was a witch... I don't know why."

Revati felt sorry for the poor chap's intelligence that was equivalent to the intelligence of a baby chimpanzee. He was very naïve, but then she realized something that he just said was little more than a revelation.

"What did you? You warned Vishu about Parvati?" Revati asked.

"Shh…" the driver's face turned grave, "Please madam, don't take her name. I am very afraid of dead people."

"But why did you warn Vishu about Parvati back in school?"

"Because he was attracted to the girl, he said he loved her…" the driver suddenly pulled the brake in an attempt to stop what he was saying. "Madam, please don't tell this to anyone. Anna doesn't like to be reminded of that past." And then he started crying like a child. She remembered Ruchika once telling her that their driver was emotionally volatile and needed to be handled with care. Shouting at him or scolding him would make him cry.

"I won't Velu. I won't!" the writer promised as she tried to wipe away the man's tears with the tissue papers lying on the dashboard. "Will you please start the car now?"

"Yes madam, I will."

Velu started the car and pressed on the accelerator until it once again exceeded the speed limits. Revati's mind was now engulfed by a new angle in the story that she was trying to decipher ever since she had come to that sleepy hill town. A new entrant who was more than just a character – it was her brother-in-law. Although she didn't want to be conclusive, but nothing stopped her from speculating the chances of it being him – the vengeful lover.

Though he had stopped crying but Velu was still sulking. His eyes were blurred out by the tears that could not flow down his eyes.

"I know they all make fun of you too. I heard Anna call you mad in front of Ruchika madam." He sulked and then continued, "But I believe you are not lying. You are not mad, and you are not the only one to hear her. I hear her too… especially in those rainy nights. She wanders in the woods, looking for her prey."

His grim words made Revati's hair stand on the end with fear. She had never expected to hear such a thing from the driver. She really wanted him to stop as it was depressing her and she did not have her Prozac tablets either.

"I am warning you, once and for all… Stay away from that witch!"

The car stopped, and Revati realized that they had reached where she wanted to go.

Central Prison, Thrissur

It was around half past ten in the morning when Revati arrived at the Central Prison in Thrissur. The Prison which is located in the Viyyur locality of the cultural capital of Kerala had a capacity of five hundred and twenty prisoners with separate sections for short-term convicts and under-trial people. Yakub was being kept in the solitary section under special orders from the Supreme Court.

The representative from the jail had received a call from the sitting MLA of the locality. Revati had her connections in the assembly because of her inclination towards the current government. The policeman opened the door and the two walked into a corridor that was very dimly lit.

"Madam, you will be wasting your time. That man hasn't spoken to any reporters in years," the policeman informed the writer who seemed very hopeful of the man in prison. "He seems to be at peace and it has pissed off many activists."

"He will talk to me, I know that," Revati said confidently.

They came to the end of the corridor and he stopped in front of a solitary confinement cell. He opened the door and paved way for Revati to enter the room.

"I will call you when your stipulated time is over. In case he does anything violent or uncalled for, just come to the door and knock it thrice," the policeman said.

Revati nodded and entered the cell. The door behind her was closed by the policeman who then waited outside.

The confinement was about twelve feet in length and a little over ten feet wide. It was dark inside except for the iron-barred window on left side wall. The light of morning sun came in through the bars and fell on the outline of what looked like a man sitting on the floor with his knees up and head rested over them. He was wearing a skullcap on his head just like they show in the news – a devout Muslim.

Revati walked two steps and then stopped. She tried to picture the face of the man who was convicted of a heinous crime.

"My name is Revati Krishna," she introduced, "I am a…"

"I know who you are…" the man interrupted rudely.

"They told me that you never talked to anyone in here."

"I don't and that's why I want you out of here," the convict warned.

"But I have not even said anything, please I want to…" Revati already started pleading.

"Seems like you couldn't complete your story," he chuckled.

"But I am not a journalist. I am here to…"

"I know who you are; You are a writer."

"How?" Revati wondered if it was appropriate to ask if the prisoner had read her books in jail.

"You told me you are a writer, how else would I know?" he asked.

"I am requesting you to talk to me. I have to know certain things. Or else it will not let me live peacefully... I know some things that have to do with you..."

"You want to know more? You want to know everything, right?" he asked without moving his head from his knees.

"I know you are innocent..." she said and then stepped forward into the light. She called him, "Yakukka!"

And for the first time he raised his head and revealed his face. He was shocked to hear the name because that was something only one person knew other than himself – and she was long dead.

Revati pulled out the necklace which she had found in the woods on the night she hallucinated about the masked man. She handed it over to Yakub. The convict who hadn't shaved his beard in years took the necklace with a trembling hand. His eyes filled up for this was a gift from him to Parvati, a gift that he had given her on that night... that doomed night.

He opened the locket and saw the picture of his beloved and asked, "How did you get this? It was lost..."

"It fell off when that monster attacked," she said sternly, "It was there all along, on that tree."

Yakub kissed the locket and held it tightly inside his palm.

"I do not have much time. I have to know things that happened that night before you were hit with the boulder," Revati requested hastily as she kneeled down in front of him.

"But you already know everything."

"What do you keep saying that I know everything and why

did you say in the beginning that you know me?" Revati asked in confusion.

"Did you forget everything or are you acting as if you do not remember?" the convict asked.

"What do you mean?"

"You came to me, in this very room, ten months ago," he revealed as his eyes pierced into hers. He continued, "You said you were writing a book and needed to know my side of the story."

Revati's pupils had dilated with fear – the fear of realizing that something was terribly wrong with her.

Yakub also realized the impending shock on her face. He inquired unassumingly, "You were expecting a baby back then, I remember. How is your child?"

Revati's eyes filled and tears streamed down her face. Now she realized what was the *story* that he mentioned when she had come into the room.

"She never got a chance to see this world of ours." Revati revealed with moist eyes.

Yakub felt sorry for the woman. He was sure that the woman would not be lying and that she indeed didn't remember anything. A brief moment of silence followed.

"It was the 24th of December, 2003..." he started narrating.

Yaqub's Statement

24 December 2003
St Augustine's Convent School

The rainy night was followed by a cloudy evening and the sky had hidden the lunar marvel under the shades of grey. There were sounds of thunder raging in the distance but the school was filled with frolic and excitement as the kids and teachers from institutions across region had gathered in a chaotic atmosphere of festivities.

It was the night of the annual inter-school fest which St. Augustine's hosted every December, right before the school closed down for the Christmas vacations. Father Tom was the principal of the school back then and he was the first person to encourage fests and extra curricular activities in the otherwise lacklustre convent school. There were songs, dances, skits, mono-acts, art exhibition and everything that the students dreamt.

While everybody was enjoying the tribal dance performance in the auditorium, I sneaked out from the green room and entered the bathroom in the ground floor. After making sure that everyone had left, I knocked on one of the doors of the toilet, and it opened. Parvati came out of the latrine with a bag full of clothes. She looked beautiful as ever. She had been hiding in closed latrine for over an hour.

"I am glad you made it!" I looked into my love's timid eyes and said.

"Of course, I had to… I was meeting you after such a long time, Yakukka…" Parvati replied. I remember the way she blushed through every word that she spoke.

"Do you know where I am going to take you?" I asked taking the bag from her.

"I will come anywhere… wherever you take me…" she had surrendered.

"I am going to take you to heaven…"

I went to the washbasin and kneeled down. That was a safe place to keep the keys to our club house. I searched underneath and then pulled out a key that I had hidden behind the ceramic neck of the washbasin. I held the girl's hand and quickly walked out of the toilet.

Few minutes later, we were walking through the woods until we reached the club house. I used the key to open the door and we went inside.

"You made a brave decision today," I said as I ran my stiff fingers through her soft hair.

"I would do anything for you, Yakukka…" she opened her heart once again for the man she loved more than anything. I knew that she felt shy and a tingling sensation passed through her navel when I touched the skin around her abdomen with my hands. She remarked shying away, "Stop doing that. Something happens to me…"

I took in a deep breath and asked, "Are you ready for it, Paru?"

The thunder raged outside.

"I… I don't know."

"It is okay, if you do not want to…" I offered if she was not ready for the tender act of making love.

"Would you be upset if I didn't want to do it?" she asked hoping that I would oblige.

"No, I won't be upset," I said smiling reassuringly.

"I love you, Yakkuka…"

And then the rain water started seeping through the gaps in the wooden ceiling and drenched us wet… and soon… we locked our lips to kiss each other. One thing led to another and before we knew it, she was on top of me. We were making love…

It was then that I heard the sounds of wet footsteps outside. Parvati had also heard it and she got cautious. She asked me to stop. Both of us pulled up our clothes. I held Parvati's hand tightly and then opened the door. I looked both sides and made sure that there was nobody. Parvati did not want to stay, so I decided that we should leave as per our plan. We had to reach Kannur, a town in the northern part of Kerala by eight in the morning, from where I was planning to elope with my Paru to the Saudi Arabia.

But then something knocked me on the head from behind. Everything around me started fading to a blur. As I fell down on my knees, I cried out to her, "Pa… P…"

I wanted her to run away as it could be anyone who didn't want us to elope, but I struggled to speak. I rested my back against a tree's trunk. In the blurred vision I could see unclearly how Parvati was looking at me clueleslly. She was scared at the possibility of someone else watching them.

"Parvati…" I managed to say finally looking into her eyes, "run for your life!"

Parvati was surprised, "Yakukka? I can't leave you like this…"

"Run!" I screamed at the top of my voice, "Don't worry about me."

And then a boulder came down and hit me on the head. I felt blood oozing out as my vision blurred into blackness.

Central Prison, Thrissur
Present day

Yakub looked out of the window as if the entire story played on a screen outside.

"And when I woke up, I found her lifeless body being taken out of the Kurmallur lake by the police. I was dragged out of the spot where I had fallen paralyzed into an ambulance. It was all a vague memory, most of it just blurred visuals and ringing sounds in my ears. I wished it was just a nightmare to which I could wake up anytime," he turned to the writer whose face showed imprints of tears that had dried up. He continued, "I was arrested because they found a torn piece from my shirt near the banks of the lake and my semen testified rape."

"But it was not a rape. You were in love," Revati stated, "Why haven't you ever told the world about this? You can be proved innocent."

"I brought her there that night. This fate was brought on her by my decision. Had she not come, she would have been alive.

Yes, maybe she would have got married to someone from her community, but she would have been alive. I must repent for my selfishness and telling the world that we made love that night would tarnish her image… so, let the world think it was rape," the lover gave a piece of his true self as he reflected the haunting event of the night in the necklace that he held in his hand.

"I had an accident nine months ago, and I lost my unborn child and husband. I understand the pain of separation."

"I am sorry to hear that."

"I do not remember coming to see you at all. The doctors have said that I am suffering from selective retrograde amnesia and that's why I have a partial loss of memory," the writer confessed. "I believed in God but after my accident I stopped believing in that unkind being in the sky who only makes people suffer." Revati said.

"I never believed in Allah," Yakub confessed, "I was just living a meaningless life. However, all these years I found refuge in the Almighty who has given me the courage to go on," Yakub said turning to Revati, "perhaps this is a test and your faith in God shall help you get to *the other side*."

Revati pondered at the possibility for a moment and then remembered something. She pulled out something from the pocket of her jeans. She held it out in front of the repenting convict and asked, "What is this?"

Yakub looked at the rusted key that Revati was holding in her hand. He started going back in time again.

The lone door of the solitary confinement started creaking as the policeman waiting outside pushed it open.

"I think this opens the…" Yakub started speaking.

"Madam, you time is up…" the policeman called out from the door that was ajar.

Revati nodded as she started showing impatience in her body language.

"What does it open?" Revati asked callously.

"It opens the club house in the woods," Yakub Ali revealed.

"Sorry madam, I will have to accompany you out," the policeman reminded in a stricter tone.

Revati got up and said looking at the necklace that Yakub was going to return, "It belongs to you, please keep it."

She turned around and started leaving.

"I loved her more than anything and I am happy that soon I will be joining her in heaven… that is of course, if Allah wills…" Yakub cried.

Revati stopped at the door when she heard the confession.

Yakub added, "I did not kill Parvati… I did not kill her…"

In a moment of fading memories, Revati turned her face and said, "I know Yakukka. I know that you didn't kill *me*…"

The word *me* sent Yakub's pulse racing. He glanced up and saw a flash of something that would drive any sane man to insanity. He saw the face of his dead lover, he saw the face of Parvati at the door.

"I will find out who killed me and justice shall be ours…" she said in a ghastly voice before turning and exiting from the door.

Yakub would have sleepless nights because he just encountered a dead person.

Ya Allah! Al-Hamdu lillah!

Revati browsed through the different folders in her smartphone. She was looking for some file that was downloaded before March 2017. She signed into a cloud storage service app through her phone and browsed further. Her eyes lit up when she noticed a file. She immediately dialled her sister on the same phone and called her.

"You would not believe me if I tell you what happened few minutes ago in the prison," Revati spoke on the phone as she sat uncomfortably in the speeding car.

"Prison? What the hell were you doing at the prison?" Ruchika asked from the other end of the phone. She was shocked to hear that Revati's important work was in prison.

"I went to meet Yakub."

"My God, you are going crazy about this episode!"

"Stop passing judgments and listen to me." The writer impatiently interjected.

"I am listening, go on…"

"Dr Gopal was right. I was aware about Yakub's side of the story, but I forgot it after the accident."

"What? How?" Ruchika asked in confusion.

"I had seen Yakub earlier this year, just before the accident. I do not remember it."

"Then how can you say that you had seen him?"

"Because Yakub remembered it. He told me that I had come to see him."

"But why did you go to see him in the first place?"

"I just checked my cloud drive on Google but it had nothing, then I remembered I also have a Skydrive installed on my phone. When I opened it I found few folders. I usually collect my notes and research documents in sky drive. There was a folder in it called *The Other Side of Her Story*," Revati disclosed something that she had also learnt few minutes back.

"Other Side of Her Story?"

"Yes, that was the title I had given to the story which I had started working on… before the accident. Remember how Aarav always wanted me to write thrillers?"

"Yes, I do."

"Well, this was supposed to be my first thriller. Yakub's story was all over the news and I was motivated to write a thriller loosely based on the murder. For this I had gone to see Yakub who had narrated his side of the story without any alteration."

"But how come your publisher never talked about this?" Ruchika asked.

"No, he didn't because I had not expressed my desire to write a thriller novel. The publisher was always against the idea, so, I was planning to write it as a screenplay for a movie. I had even met the director. Only three people knew about this- Aarav, me and Yakub." Revati clarified.

Ruchika thought for a moment and then said, "So, that's how you picked up the name *Parvati*."

"Yes, I believe so."

The car went up a speed breaker at such a high speed that Revati's head almost bumped on to the ceiling. Her phone fell down.

"Velu, could you please slow down, I am not in a hurry to reach the school, please," she requested the driver as she bent to pick up the phone from below the seat.

"I am sorry, madam," Velu apologized and slowed down.

The phone was back in Revati's hand and she placed it on her right ear as usual.

"What happened, what was the commotion about?" Ruchika asked anxiously.

"Speed breaker!"

"That idiot doesn't understand when to slow down. You should scold him." Ruchika instructed.

"That's okay. He understood and won't do it again," Revati said calmly.

Ruchika got back to their conversation, "So, does this mean that you are actually accepting the fact that you are mentally ill?"

"Well, the doctor's diagnosis seems correct, but…"

"… but?"

"But there are certain things which no one could have known which I know…"

"It could be possible that someone must have told but you don't remember," Ruchika tried to debate.

"That someone is dead. It is Parvati?" Revati answered, "I think there is one person who could help us now."

"Who's that?"

"The one person who knows the school inside out – Father Joseph. I will ask him to get me old records of students from Parvati's batch."

"I think he would be helpful, you should ask. Though he is very caught up with the fest activities."

"Yes, I know. I will be there at the school in another thirty minutes. I will see him after that," Revati said and hung up the phone.

Outnumbered by the questions that kept popping up in the writer's mind, she tried to concentrate on her breathing. She tried to meditate but she kept recalling the club house from Yakub's story

"Velu…" she called.

"Yes, madam?" the driver answered politely.

"Do you know anything about the club house?"

"Ayyo! I don't know much but I have heard about it," he said in disgust.

"What sort of things have you heard about it?" She tried to know.

"It was a place where school boys used to go to smoke. There were the rebel boys from outside who would come to supply *ganja* to senior students. It was a bad place, madam," he revealed. "No good boy goes to that place, only bad boys went there. You should not go there."

"I won't," Revati replied.

Although she said that she won't go to the club house, she knew that that was exactly the place she must visit.

"Madam?"

"Yes, Velu," Revati responded to the driver.

"Can I take a half-day tomorrow?"

"But tomorrow we have the fest. You will be needed."

"My father is not keeping well. I have to take him to the hospital in the morning. But I will be there in the second half, I promise."

"You should ask Ruchika, right?"

"She will not give me half-day. She never understands. Could you please talk to her?" The driver pleaded with half-filled eyes.

Revati felt sorry for the poor chap. She knew very well that her sister was nothing short of Hitler. She took pity in Velu's plight and gently patted him on the shoulder.

"It is okay, Velu. You can take the whole day off. I will talk to Ruchika," she assured him.

Velu smiled and thanked the kind writer. For a moment Revati's worries were forgotten as she thought about the poverty-ridden driver's condition. He was still smiling despite all his pain, like a child unaware of the cruel world that existed outside his innocent world. She wished she could also be like him, and forget about all the pain and negativity in life. But sadly she wasn't. She was a writer, and she thought more about the morose than the morose.

Few minutes later, she was dropped outside the front gate of the school. She got out of the car and went inside the school to meet Father Joseph.

12 noon
St Augustine's

Revati walked into the principal's office. She forgot to knock on the door before entering, rather she did not care to follow protocol. She had much more important things running in her mind, with questions that were strangling her with an intangible hand from the inside of her mind.

The principal expected all his staff to arrive at 6:30 am at the school, exactly one hour before the assembly, so that they can be prepared for the day ahead. However, Revati was entering at noon. Something that didn't go well with the principal.

"Well, well... Look who's here!" the father exclaimed without looking at the entrant.

"Good morning, Father..."

"Good afternoon, Mrs Revati Krishna," he interrupted as he tapped on his watch and asked, "Seems like punctuality doesn't run in the family," he commented, "I guess it is matriarchal."

"Sorry father. I... I have to talk to you about something. It is urgent."

"Is it related to the fest or your class?" he asked.

"No… not really!"

"Then it can wait."

"But father this…"

Again he interrupted the writer dimwittedly, "I understand that you must have brought forth something important to you but I am very occupied at the moment with the fest on my head, I don't think I can attend to your personal issues."

Revati felt sad at the man's response but she also understood the fact that organizing a fest that would bring over a thousand students together was a tedious task. She walked back to the door. The entire conversation with Yakub was playing back and forth inside her head and those were topped up by the questions that she was asking herself. The dilemma was evident on the woman's face that was crumpling to the pressure.

Father Joseph was a little disappointed at the late coming but then he felt terrible for being so inconsiderate to the writer who was going through so much. He sighed and dropped his glasses on the table. He was a man of faith, and it was the message of his God to help those who are in need.

"We can talk after lunch at the dance room," he said softly.

"Thank you, Father."

"1:30, not a minute late," he stated clearly, "I believe that you have a class at 12."

Revati nodded and left the room.

Indeed, Revati had a class at 12. She had already missed her morning lecture and hell must have broken loose in the class of Eleventh Section C. She hurried across the corridor and reached the staircase near the abandoned toilet on the ground floor. While panting to the class she felt like she just heard something from inside the toilet on the way. She stopped for a moment. She stepped aside and placed her ear to the wall.

"Hey, there is no key here," a boy said from inside the toilet.

"It is okay. I have a spare key. Let's go before someone catches us," another boy replied.

"You have the stuff, right?"

"It is at the club house, now come, let's go!"

And then there was the sound of the door opening, Revati made sure that she was not seen by hiding behind the wall. When she came a little forward she noticed that one of the two boys was Muthu from her class. Intrigued by the new information that she had learnt, Revati followed the boys to the back of the school. The huge football ground ended with a wide fence that cumulated at an outhouse. It was supposedly the old sports room, but hardly anyone used it. The boys had gone behind the sports room. Revati also tiptoed and went behind the room. The gap between the back wall of the room and the fence was claustrophobically small. But one of the wooden planks of the fence vibrated as if it was moved minutes ago. She touched and then gently pushed it, and the plank swung like a pendulum. It was an opening to world beyond, to the dark woods of Kurmallur.

Revati trudged through the muddy ground, dodging branches that were swinging towards her. She had lost the boys but there was something that kept whispering the way into her ears.

After some time, she sighted a wooden cabin that did not have a proper roof. It was poorly constructed and she could see smoke rising up from the semi-open ceiling. The smell of tobacco blended with marijuana spread into the moist odour of the woods and tinkled her nostrils. She was shocked at the kind of things kids were doing.

It was a bad place, madam. Velu had said in the car. *No good boy goes to that place; only bad boys went there. You should not go there.*

Revati realized that the driver had been right. It was indeed a place where dirty rotten scoundrels would go and she got a strange sensation. A sensation to pray to God for protection. The last time she had prayed while in the car with Aarav, but that prayer shook her faith in God. As she took a step, she accidentally broke a branch of the tree. The kids inside the club house got alerted and ran from the other side.

The kids left the place with silence. The sound of wings fluttering was heard above the club house, shortly followed by the cawing of the crow. Revati acknowledged the presence of the intruder and started her journey towards the club house.

But somebody else was watching her from far away.

The Club House, Kurmallur

The air inside the club house was intoxicating but somehow she felt more in control of her mind than otherwise. She wondered if it was the effect of the marijuana. The club house was more like a dumping ground for old items. There were three stools – two of them broken and a small table that had one missing leg. On the floor lay a carom board which seemed like a regular venue for games. On the corner of room was a trunk box that was probably used as a seat by the smokers who came in there.

Outside, someone was approaching the club house stealthily like a snake eyeing its prey.

Inside, Revati kneeled down before the trunk and noticed that it was locked. She checked the lock. She pulled out the rusted key from her pocket. It fitted perfectly into the keyhole of the lock. She turned it, though the rust did get in the way, but then it unlocked the trunk. With her heart pounding for clues, she opened the trunk.

The sound of leaves rustling could be heard outside as Revati found lots of old stuff inside the trunk box. Pictures, magazines, articles, yearbooks etc. While going through the photos, she came across a particular group photo of three boys that shocked her. In the photo, one of the boys was not wearing any mask and looking straight, the second one was without a mask but looking behind, and third one was wearing mask. She could identify the mask which she had been seeing in her nightmarish visions – the mask of the killer.

The door opened and someone came inside scaring the writer who was already nervous. She recoiled in shock as the photos and other artifacts fumbled from her hands into the floor.

"Revati?" It was the voice of Father Joseph.

Revati got up from the floor of the room, automatically sending the trunk door to close, which created a thudding sound.

"Thank God, it is you!" Revati relaxed upon noticing that it was Father Joseph who had come inside.

"What are you doing here? I saw you leaving towards the sports room, so immediately followed you," Father Joseph explained in a concerned tone.

"I followed some boys," Revati replied.

"I know who all come here. Do you know how dangerous it is for you to be here?"

"Yes, I know."

"A girl was raped and murdered in these woods. You are well informed about it."

"I think, it was the same girl's spirit that brought me here," Revati remarked.

"What nonsense?" the father asked agitatedly.

"I wouldn't have believed it either but it is happening to me."

"Would you mind talking about it in the school. We should not stay here," the pastor advised as he started walking.

"Of course, Father!' Revati moved out and joined him. She pressed the photograph inside her pocket.

As they trekked out of the woods, she felt a sense of deja-vu again. It was difficult for her not to note down the resemblance to the incident that had happened here in the long forgotten past.

"What are you trying to prove, Revati?" asked Father Joseph.

"I... I..." the writer stammered as she did not know how to put her thoughts in to words, for the first time in her life.

"Small towns like ours have secrets, deeply buried... Why are you trying to unearth that buried secret which might cost your life?"

"Father, I believe that if I don't do what I need to do, then it will cost an innocent's life."

They reached the backside of the school. The pastor held the plank and allowed Revati to go inside first. After that he followed. They passed the sports room and were on route to the dance room.

"You are not saving anyone's life. You are only endangering your own life," Joseph said.

"I went to see Yakub Ali in the morning..."

"What? Why?" the father appeared shocked.

"Because Parvati wanted me to see him."

"My dear, Parvati died in 2003... that man whom you went to meet killed her..."

"She has shown me a lot and when I met Yakub, I got convinced that he did not kill her."

All these talks about souls and murder was scaring the holy man. Although he did not want to concede it in front of the writer. He was glad that he entered the school premise which was built on holy ground.

As Joseph entered the dance hall he asked the writer, "If he did not kill her then who did?"

"That is exactly what Parvati's undead spirit is trying to seek through me," revealed Revati.

"There was enough evidence to prove that Yakub killed her." The principal argued softly.

"Yakub was with her and they had shared intimate moments together, but he never raped or murdered her," Revati said confidently. "The real killer is still roaming freely."

"Jesus Christ! From being a rational person who argued about the existence of God, today you are talking about souls and spirits!" he sighed, "If you think that you are possessed or haunted by a soul then I know a good exorcist in Kochi. If you want, I can…"

"Don't! A girl who suffered rape and treachery, moments before being murdered cannot be evil. If there is a God, then hers shall be done…"

"Mrs Revati Krishna, you need divine help. Stay here, let me get something that might help you. Could you please wait for me here in this room?" asked Father Joseph.

"Yes, Father," she replied and sat on the chair.

Father Joseph smiled and left the dance room. Revati on the other hand tried to relax.

She looked at all the trophies and medals that the school had won in various dance competitions. There were over a dozen framed pictures of prize winners sporting their medals on various occasions. Intrigued by the pictures, she got up to look at them one by one.

The school's highlight had been the group folk dance competition. They had won at state level continuously between 1999 and 2003. The group that won gold in those five years specialized in a western fusion of Theyyam and Kathakali, two traditional dance forms of Kerala. In 2004 however, they had a medal but it was a solo performance in the traditional form of the dance. She looked carefully at the picture, it was of a young boy of nineteen with a gold medal in his neck and body painted red. He was holding the medal to the neck with his right hand, however, there was something in his left hand too that was partly hidden behind his costume. Revati looked closely and realized that it was the mask that had been haunting her. Her heart skipped a beat. She searched for some kind of a manual that enlisted prize winners on the table. She finally got a yearbook which had the names of all winners and contestants of the year 2004. With every beat that her heart produced, her breath got heavier. She opened the yearbook to the page that had the names of the dance participants. With her finger she went through the names until her eyes hit the name of the winner in Men's Solo Dance Competition which was printed at the bottom in bold ink.

"Alfred…" Revati read as her eyes popped out in disbelief. Revati's nerves froze and her heart stopped almost beating. With all her might, she ran out of the room.

Revati rushed into the music room where she caught Ruchika by surprise. She dragged her sister by the hand and led her to a corner in the corridor.

"I know who did it!" Revati said panting.

"Who?" Ruchika was intrigued to know.

"The man behind the mask was Alfred – the school's most famous dancer during his time." She paused to take a breath and then continued, "The boy whose influence that Parvati didn't like was an Alfred… she had mentioned in her journal."

"You got her journals? From where?" Ruchika asked with shock.

"Shh… that's not important now. The important thing is the fact that the boy who went on to become the principal of the very school where he studied was Father Joseph."

She paused for stress and then pronounced each word with vengeance, *"Father Alfred Joseph!"*

"No way!" Ruchika recoiled in disbelief.

"Did he become a priest because he couldn't live with the guilt of murdering an innocent girl?" Revati tried to deduce but then she had another thought, "Did he become a priest to cover up his wrongdoings? So, that nobody suspects him of murder?"

"But… do you have any proof other than your so-called intuitions?" Ruchika asked.

Revati came out of her adventurous plight and perceived the fact that she did not have any tangible proof against the unholy priest.

"Look, I think we should try to get him to confess. That's the only way I think we can do something about it," Revati concluded.

And then they heard a girl screaming from the dance room. Revati and Ruchika along with other students sprinted to the source of the scream. A group of students had already assembled in the dance room, surrounding something that was lying on the floor. Revati inched further and the sight of the *thing* lying on the floor gave her chills.

The body of Father Alfred Joseph lay on the floor drenched in blood, lifeless and dead.

6 p.m.
Kurmallur Police Station

After the gruesome murder of Father Joseph, everyone at the school was detained by the police. After the initial investigation, a handful of them were asked to report at the local police station for interrogation. After waiting for hours at the waiting area, Revati was finally summoned by Inspector Sebastian for a formal session.

"Do you have any idea as to who or why Father Joseph was killed?" the inspector asked in a milder tone because of the heavy load respect that he had for the writer.

"Inspector, I am stunned at Joseph's murder. At the moment I cannot answer your question," Revati replied thoughtfully.

"There are eye witnesses, mostly students, who have testified that they had seen you coming with Father Joseph from the football ground. And you also accompanied him," he paused to pick up the statement issued by students and read it, "to the dance room. You were the last person to be seen with the priest."

"Yes, I was. I had gone to seek help."

"Yes, I heard about your mental condition, Mrs Revati."

Revati rolled back on her chair in wonderment.

"Don't be so surprised. This is a small town – talks and rumors hardly stay within walls," Sebastian explained.

"I had gone to seek help because I wanted to know something about Parvati Subramaniam from him," the writer spoke boldly in her defense.

Sebastian felt an irritation when she said that. He slapped his forehead with his palm and said, "Here we go again!"

"Listen, I think I know who killed Parvati Subramaniam," Revati claimed.

"Yes, of course! Everyone knows that Yakub killed her."

"No! It was not Yakub…"

"How can you say that? There is evidence that Yakub killed her. We found his semen in…"

"There was evidence that he was with her, maybe in an intimate act of love… which you and media have termed 'rape'…" she fought on. "I know what I am going to say will not make any sense to you… It did not make any sense to me either, in the beginning… But I am being guided by the spirit of Parvati…"

"Revati…" he tried to interrupt.

"Please do not look at me with that sympathy… I don't need it. I am completely sane. In fact, I haven't felt this need to live since my husband and baby died. Parvati's spirit has given me a reason to live and to seek the truth… And when I met Yakub…"

"You what…?" Inspector asked expressing his disbelief.

"I met him early this morning…"

"What exactly are you trying to prove? That we police officers and the forensic experts are buffoons? Or are you also trying to make a mockery of our judiciary so that a bunch of journalists can make sensational stories about the system's inefficiency?"

"Did you know that I have been living in the same house where once Parvati used to live… in the same room?" Revati got up from her seat in a heated reaction. She continued, "Did you know that there is a secret compartment above the ceiling on the first floor in which some of the old stuff belonging to Parvati were kept?" She pulled out some pictures and the journal and placed it on the table in front of the inspector, "Look, I found these in that compartment."

Sebastian picked up the letters and photo. He went through it carefully.

"It is Parvati's personal writings. Nobody has ever seen them until now. The last thing that she wrote was on 24th December 2003…'

"The very night that she was murdered," Sebastian realized.

"And she has mentioned that she was going to see Yakub in the woods that night."

"So, even if he had sex with her, this could be used as proof in the court of law ward off the rape charges." Sebastian said as he quickly glanced through the contents of that particular writing.

"And she has mentioned particularly about one Alfred in her journal. Someone who stalked her… a scoundrel. Until today I did not know who he was…But then I saw his picture in the school," Revati said.

Sebastian looked up at her seeking the name, rather proof to support her allegation. Revati had already prepared the photo that she had found in the club house and placed it in front of the police inspector.

"It was Father Joseph... Father Alfred Joseph... When I came here, I had visions where I saw a figure in mask. I did not what was going on. Until I saw this picture…"

"That's Joseph…" he said and then carefully scanned the other teenager in the photo. There was a spark of recognition a moment later and he said, "and that's Vishwanathan, I mean Vishu."

"Yes, they were part of the same dance group. Yakub was also in the same group. Together they had won in men's group dance for a continuous period of five years until 2003 when the group fell apart because of Yakub's absence," Revati further stated her theory.

"Who is this third one? The face is blurred."

"I bet it is Yakub," Revati said confidently. "Inspector, I am telling you that I suspected Father Joseph, and I rushed out of the room the moment I saw that picture on the wall… I was going to come to you…"

"But if he was the killer, then why did someone else kill him? What was he hiding?"

"The identity of the killer," Revati added, "Since Yakub is in jail, there is someone else involved. Someone who has been free for all this time while Yakub suffered silently in jail."

The inspector got up from his seat and walked to the shelf where a carton was kept. He wore a plastic glove in his right hand and with it he pulled out a thick book from inside and placed it on the table. It was a copy of the Bible that had semi-dry stains of blood.

"We found this Bible in Joseph's hand. Do you know why he must have held on to it?" the inspector inquired.

"He mentioned that I needed divine help. He asked me to stay in the room as he went inside the store room to get something that might help me," Revati said remembering the final words Joseph had said before he departed from that room. She inferred, "Joseph believed that I was emotionally weak and he had said that he wanted to help me. He left after I agreed to take his help. Maybe this was his way of…" she bickered a little and then said, "No, I am not… I don't trust that man anymore."

"His finger was placed inside the book and it pressed on to a particular verse from Leviticus. This one." Sebastian said as he opened the holy book to a page that had a verse highlighted with Joseph's blood.

"And he that kills any man shall surely be put to death," Revati read from the book.

"Does that mean anything to you?" the inspector tried to know.

"A last minute effort to justify his sin?"

"Or it could simply point to Yakub… the man who killed Parvati, being put to death by law… tomorrow…"

"No, it is not Yakub. Yakub wanted her to escape that night."

"You can't believe what Yakub told you. He could be lying," Sebastian argued as he took the Bible back and closed it.

"I know, because I saw it happening in front of my eyes. When I read Parvati's writings and poems, I realized how deeply the two were in love. Inspector, this is not a story of revenge," the soft hair on the edge of her arm stood up and she said, "This is a story of undying love…"

"Mrs Revati, I want to believe you because I have always believed in every word that you have written in your books. But these are very loose ramblings that are not substantial evidence."

"Believe me, Yakub did not kill her!" the writer pleaded.

"If it was not Yakub or Joseph… then who could…" Before the inspector could complete his question, someone enters the room without permission.

"Inspector Sebastian…" the man said.

Inspector Sebastian looked at the incoming man and smiled, "Vishu, please have a seat."

"Thank you, but I am in a hurry. I am here to take my sister-in-law home. You and I both know that she has not done it." Vishu was in such a haste that he did not even bother to smile back.

"Of course, would you please give me a moment. She will have to sign some papers before she could leave," Sebastian said and handed over a form from his drawer. He informed, "Please make sure that you are present any time we summon you for an interrogation or identification.'

"Look, Sebastian. I do not want any trouble for her. She is not keeping well," Vishu hissed with a straight face.

"These are just standard protocols."

Revati and Vishu signed on the papers and then in the register.

"I hope that is all," Vishu said bluntly and turned to Revati and called her, "Let's go."

Without saying anything else, Vishu left the room. He seemed to be in great hurry. Revati courteously looked at Sebastian before she left the room after her brother-in-law.

Sebastian picked up the form that was signed by Revati and Vishu. He filed it in a folder and kept it inside his drawer. He looked at the Bible that was still lying in front of him.

And he that kills any man shall surely be put to death.

The verse from Leviticus stared at him mockingly as if the book was challenging him to solve a riddle. The inspector sat in his chair and took the book in his hand. There was definitely more to this than what met the eye.

It had started to rain outside amidst sounds of thunder.

It had started drizzling and the setting sun had left an orange sky for the eyes to see. The four-wheeler cruised on an empty road. Inside Vishu was talking on the phone with his wife while Revati was lost in investigative thoughts.

"Yes, I will halt at Trisha's place and pick up Kriti," Vishu grumbled on the phone.

"How could you even forget?" Ruchika complained from the other end of the line.

"Velu forgot to pick her up." The husband complained nonchalantly.

"That idiot is worthless. He can't remember a thing!" the wife angrily yelled on the phone.

"Moreover, I did not want her to see Revati coming out from the police station. It was better to pick her up after I picked up your crazy sister," he passed a taunt on Revati.

"Fine! Just pick her up and come, otherwise you are all staying outside. One has gone insane and other one doesn't care about his daughter. I am done with this family!" she said and hung up the phone.

Ruchika, though on phone, her voice was very loud and both Velu and Revati could hear it. Revati felt sorry but then she was determined to find out the truth, while Vishu was truly irritated. He could not take it anymore. When Ruchika had first told Vishu that she would be bringing her sister to stay with them, he did not object because he did not expect her to be a crack-case. He belonged to the one of the most influential families in the town and had his reputation at stake because of a mad woman living with him. And on top that, he had lost a dear friend – Alfred Joseph.

"You know, Joseph was a nice guy," he clarified, "Although he was a little messed up during school days, but those who knew him personally knew how much of a gem he was."

There was no response from the writer which further fueled Vishu's irritation.

"He was a close friend of mine back in those days. I know, he would do many notorious things like smoking and drinking in the woods but he would never kill someone," Vishu added, "Ruchika told me that you suspected Joseph…"

Revati interrupted her brother-in-law's defense, "The killer wore a mask and his body was painted in red. When I saw that picture of Joseph in the dance room, I was hundred percent sure that he is the masked killer. But then…"

Revati paused to put things together in her head because something was not making sense. She said, "The killer is out there, free to roam!"

"Why do you want to get involved in all this mess? You came to chill, just write your fucking novel and leave." Vishu was agitated. He tried to calm down and said, "Why are you putting your life in danger for someone you don't even know?"

"I am doing it for the soul of a girl who awaits justice, and being a woman who has lost everything, I have nothing to fear or lament about…" stated Revati.

Just then the car stopped in the middle of the road.

"What happened, Velu?" Vishu asked.

"I will check Vishu anna," Velu said obediently and got out of the car. He pulled open the bonnet.

Turning to Revati, Vishu said, "It would be good if you stopped this and went back to Gurgaon."

"Why do you want me to stay away from the truth? It could actually save your friend from getting hung for no crime of his own."

"Yakub is not my friend. He is a killer and he should be punished."

"Why are you trying to save the killer?" Revati asked with a dewy eye.

"I am only trying to save you, dear."

"Unless…" Revati's moist eyes turned white in horror.

Revati opened the door and came outside, as if repelling from the man inside the car. Vishu also got out trying to calm the insane sister-in-law.

"Revati, wait… what are you doing?" He called the woman who was frantically looking towards the woods on the left side of the highway.

"Stay away from me…" she warned.

A confused Velu walked past to the dickie to pick up a spanner so that he could repair the car's broken engine. He wondered what was going on.

Revati walked further away from Vishu. She took the mobile phone out of her pocket and dialled Ruchika's number, but no one answered the call. She turned around to check if Vishu was following, but to her surprise, there was no one.

And suddenly a pair of hands came from behind and started choking her. The writer desperately attempted to free herself from his grip. She struggled, but kept her mobile phone inside her pocket. Soon, the world in front of her faded into black, and then her eyes closed.

Kurmallur Police Station

Sebastian's head ached but he tried to focus on the finer details and fingerprints in the Bible that the deceased Joseph was holding on to at the time of his death.

And he that kills any man shall surely be put to death.

The verse echoed like a Gregorian chant in his head. It was something that he had grown up hearing. When he was eight years old he had been a regular at the Bible classes. He was the one who was the most interested in the book. He always wanted to know about what happened after death. When the nun who took the classes told little Sebastian about heaven and hell, his mind was fixated on hell.

That day in the Bible class, a seven-year-old Sebastian had asked, "Did man have the right to send someone to hell?"

"And he that kills any man shall surely be put to death," replied the nun and revealed, "Leviticus 24:17." The nun had quoted from the Old Testament.

As he thought of that incident from the past he wondered if Yakub was indeed innocent like Revati claimed, then would all people who are responsible for his hanging be sent to hell.

And he that kills any man shall surely be put to death –
Leviticus 24:17.

He remembered the words of the nun as he looked at the highlighted verse. Then it caught his attention – *Leviticus* 24:17.

He started flipping the pages and stopped at page 24. He ran his index finger down the page until he reached seventeenth line.

He noticed something scribbled with a ball pen.

Stay away from V.........N.

Splattered blood hid the letters between V and N.

Joseph had wanted to warn Revati but he could not do it directly because he knew he was being watched by someone. Who could it be? The inspector started thinking.

Sebastian remembered the photo that Revati had shown earlier which she found in the club house.

That's Joseph… and **Vishu**. He had identified looking at the faces. *Joseph's full name was Alfred Joseph. While Vishu's full name was Vishwanathan Iyer.*

"Oh my God! That's what Joseph wanted to tell Revati – *Stay away from Vishwanathan…*"

The very next moment, the inspector's mobile got a notification. He unlocked the screen with his left thumb and saw that there was an incoming SoS on the Nirbhaya app.

Five minutes before.
Kurmallur forest

The sweet smell of wild grass and wet soil entered her nostrils. Revati's eyelashes moved nonchalantly as the cursed rays of light entered her eyes creating an unclear illusion of a vision. Drops of drizzling rain covered her eyes.

Her head felt unusually heavy and her body was numb. However, she could infer that she was being moved. With great effort she tilted her dizzy head towards the left and she noticed a hand holding her by the collar of her shirt and dragging mercilessly over the muddy ground of the woods. A sudden gush of pain passed through her veins as the stones and thorns on the ground rubbed and pierced through her back.

Run Parvati… run!

Yakub had said that night to Parvati. Had she run away she would have not died in the hands of this dreaded psycho. The psycho who was dragging the writer to the place where he had finished the girl fifteen years ago.

Revati wished that the innocent Parvati had run away. She could hear the sounds from that night. And the rain drops falling on her gave her the sensation that Parvati had felt on that unfateful night.

They reached the shore of the lake and the dragging of Revati's body stopped. The hand let go of her shirt's collar. Revati tried to move but it was very difficult, but still she managed to turn around and get on her knees. She started looking up.

"Everything was going well..." said the man who stood towering in front of the writer, "I started over!"

Revati tried to focus on the man's face as her ocular muscles adjusted to bring the blurred face in focus. The voice was familiar, but the tone and pitch were different.

"But then a writer from a big city arrives in the small town and starts digging out all those graves that I had covered up so carefully," he snarled in a hissing voice.

Revati was struggling to maintain balance on her knees.

The man grabbed and lifted her by the hair. She yelled in pain.

"Why did you have to come here, Revati..." he paused as he came closer to her face, "...madam?"

Revati saw the face and it sent a curling electric impulse down her knees.

"Ve... Velu?" the writer asked with her dried up lips.

"The name is Velappan Mathews, son of Vincent Mathews!" He declared like a triumphant villain and let go off her hair, sending the writer down on her face. His voice was the same but it was the way he spoke that differed. He was not speaking like a pleading child anymore.

"Perhaps everything happens for a reason. This guilt has been piling up in my head and I wanted to confess this many times, but could not do it. But I think I can do it now before you, after all, you are not going to be of any danger to me after tonight. It is going to be your last night."

He had brought a rope tied to his waist. He caught hold of Revati's ankle and tied the rope around it.

"That night," he began narrating, "after the performance, Joseph and I were supposed to go to the club house where I had hidden some *ganja*. Yes, he was a regular. I was always the backup dancer of the group so I was dressed up in the red dress and waiting for Joseph backstage. After the performance, I saw Yakub and Parvati elope into the woods. I went after them only to see them naked on top of each other. I had never seen a woman naked in my life other than my mother, but that was when I was little. For the first time in my life, I got a sensation so terrifying that I could not control it. It was a tingling sensation that burnt me inside like a fire in a confiscated hearth. What was worse was that it was that bastard who was enjoying the girl's body. I started burning with envy," Velu clenched his teeth as he started dragging the rope tied to Revati towards the lake.

"I picked up a boulder and threw it on Yakub. What else could I do? I wanted that woman. Do you know how soft her body felt? Like butter."

"And then with all my might I pushed Parvati towards that tree. I wanted to do what Yakub was doing to her. I bet it felt nice, in and out… in and out…" the insane driver chuckled like the devil. "But Parvati was like a timid fawn. She tried to defend herself and ran but she fell and hit her head on the same boulder which I had used to knock out Yakub. I did not want to kill her but before I knew she died. I heard footsteps approaching and in that moment I got tense. It was Joseph who came in at that time… He saw me doing it…"

Velu tied the loose end of the rope to the boulder that was lying on the shore of the lake.

"I told Joseph that he would meet the same fate if he did not keep quiet. Besides I knew enough secrets about him, so he had to oblige. The son of a bitch was not even fit to be a priest. All these years he kept the guilt inside until that day when he was going to confess to you. But I didn't let it happen."

"You… killed Joseph?" Revati asked in fits of breathlessness.

"He didn't deserve to live. I am sure he must have reached hell by now. Whatever you say, he gave a hand in pushing that boulder into the lake," Velu said as he started pushing the heavy boulder towards the lake.

The drizzle had started turning into heavier downpour. The orange of the sunset had turned to a hellish red sky.

"And once again history repeats itself. I did not hate you because you were always nice to me. But I have to remove anyone who comes between me and my freedom. That includes Joseph, you," Velu paused to take a breath. He said, "And Vishu as well… He was a good man, like an elder brother. He was a little proud of his family heritage, but that's okay. I hate his wife, that whore Ruchika. I would love to get my hands on her after this, and then that kid. You know I have her in the car's dickie." He chuckled again, "She will be chopped into pieces after everything is done. All of you will be dealt with separately, but tomorrow's headlines will be something like this, "Insane writer turns psycho, kills her family and jumps into lake and commits suicide," the driver said as if reading out from an invisible newspaper.

"You bastard!" Revati cried in disgust.

"Now, I am thinking if I should throw you just like that or if I should also get the taste of your body. It has been long, you know…" he came closer to her and hissed. "Fifteen years since I touched a woman."

He ripped the writer's shirt and the three top buttons were sent off in the air like balls coming out of a canon.

"I will leave you satisfied *sexually* before you die of drowning. Just like your ghost. Where is your ghost? I am really sorry that your ghost did not come to save you," he mocked the dead and laughed.

"Or maybe I will just push you into the lake and dig inside your sister's body." The psycho got second thoughts. "Yes, that would be better. She is more voluptuous, you know."

He pushed the boulder into the lake with his right foot. "Goodbye… Revati *madam*!"

There was a huge splash as the boulder went into the water. The rope went swiveling down like the drill-bit of an extremely powerful drilling machine. And finally the rope pulled the writer into the chilling waters of the lake.

The déjà vu of drowning in the water brushed by her murderously as she struggled to stay near the surface. A cold pair of hands came inside the water and grabbed her neck. She had given up her fight as the water entered her lungs. It was all closing down – the sight, the sounds, the sensations. She was dying. She saw the beautiful face of Parvati Subramaniam in front of her eyes before it faded into the blackness of death. Her body had a lightness and she felt like she was going up towards heaven.

Five minutes later

Something was pushing into her stomach and making her spit the excess water out of her system. She could see someone leaning on his knees, but her ears were still mute. She coughed a little more and sat up on the ground. It was Inspector Sebastian. He gave a gentle smile and helped her get up. She saw that there were couple of constables who were arresting Velu.

"H... how?" Revati asked in between breaths.

Sebastian showed him his mobile on the screen of which the *Nirbhaya* app was opened. He explained, "I got your SoS, and everything he said has been recorded in the conversation."

"Vishw..."

"Vishu was knocked down near the car. Velu had hit him on his head before he came to you. He survived the hit and is conscious now."

Suddenly she remembered something that Velu had said in his confession. The writer held the inspector's shirt and got up.

"He has kidnapped Kriti too..." Revati said nervously.

'We heard him say that so we checked the dickie of your car. Your niece was found unconscious. She has been taken to the hospital with Vishu. Both of them should be alright. You have nothing to worry," the inspector assured, "Come, let us take you to the hospital too," he said looking at the bruises and cuts on her body.

Sebastian helped the writer walk to the police vehicle that was parked on the highway. Right behind them, the constables were bringing Velu. His nose was bleeding probably from the punch he must have received from Sebastian when the police arrived at the spot using the GPS location sent by Revati's mobile app. Revati turned and looked at the disgusting face of the driver who was spitting venom from his dark aura. She turned ahead and limped her way to the police vehicle.

But then the inspector heard a gunshot from behind. Sebastian turned and saw that one of his men were down on the ground while Velu was holding the constable's revolver. He shot the other constable and then was quick enough to send a bullet into Sebastian's chest. The inspector tumbled down in pain. Then Velu pointed the revolver at Revati.

"None of you will live. I promise you that..." Velu hissed, "the price of my freedom."

He shot another bullet into Sebastian's elbow and one into his thigh. He writhed in pain.

"Looks like, we have to say goodbye again." His finger latched on to the trigger.

Revati looked at him helplessly. She wanted to run but she could hardly stand on her own. Sebastian's phone had the evidence. If Velu stole that and ran away, then she wouldn't be able to save Yakub from hanging. She closed her eyes and prayed. She prayed once again to the God whom she had prayed when she was in the car with Aarav while going to meet his parents.

Oh Lord Krishna, I beg you to keep me alive till I hand over this evidence which would prove Yakub innocent and set Parvati's spirit free... Please, that is my only wish...

He was about to pull the trigger when the intruder flew in with its pitch black wings and landed on the psycho's face. It landed with its claws piercing into his eyes and sunk its beak in Velu's right ear. Velu tried hard to get rid of the crow. He tried to hit it but he missed and hit his own face instead. The gun fell from his and landed on the mud.

The crow had always shown the way, and Revati remembered what Velu had said when she entered Ruchika's house.

Ayyo! No madam. Please do not drive away crows. They are the departed souls of loved ones.

"You were wrong, Velu," she said looking at the killer who was being punished by the intruder for his doings, "Crows are not the departed souls. They are the souls who could never depart, because of people like you."

As Velu screamed in pain, Sebastian got up with great struggle. He witnessed what could only be part of a horror novel or movie. An ending where everything fails but nature herself chooses to punish the guilty. However, as a person of law, it was his duty to arrest the killer. So, he picked up the constable's revolver that Velu had stolen from the mud and caught hold of him. The crow hovered over the killer's head and started ascending. Velu was bleeding from all parts of his upper body.

Revati looked at the crow. People may never believe it, but she would know forever that it was the girl's soul that had guided her in the form of a crow. The crow gave one last look towards Revati and then flew into the dark sky.

4:50 am, The Next Morning
Thrissur Central Prison

It was the day of the execution. Yakub got ready for his final namaaz of this life on earth. He did not feel any regret but he was eagerly waiting to join his lover in heaven, if Allah willed. A bucket of water was kept in the corner of the room for his *Ghusl* before he performed *Fajr*. He sat next to the bucket and was about to wash his body when he heard something near the barred window of his confinement.

He looked towards the window, but there was no one but the darkness before dawn that crept through the clouds. He looked back towards the bucket and dipped his hand in the water. He saw a spectre of light reflecting on the surface of the water. He immediately got up and turned around to witness what was nothing short of a miracle.

A glowing spectre of white light had formed inside his cell, and in the lap of the spectre was the moon like figure of Parvati. She looked brighter than ever, and as pure as an angel. Indeed, she had arrived with the angels.

He walked towards the spectre and stood face to face with the apparition of his dead lover. Parvati smiled and Yakub smiled back while his eyes streamed rivers of tears.

And then he heard the sound of the door opening. His attention faltered, but then he realized that there was nothing in the room but him. The policeman had opened the door and come inside.

"Is it time?" Yakub asked.

The policeman did not respond.

"I would request you to let me perform my final prayer," the convict requested humbly.

"You may finish your prayer, and you will have many more days to pray after this," the policeman said.

"What? What do you mean?"

"It means that God is kind and has some strange ways to give justice after all. The real killer confessed last evening. It is all over the news. There has been a special plea to postpone your hanging, and your lawyers are holding an emergency meeting with the President of our country as we speak."

Yakub looked at him in shock. First the apparition of his lover and now this news about finding the real killer.

"That crazy writer was not crazy after all. She is the one who found the real killer," the policeman smiled and concluded, "Please carry on with your prayers. God has heard them for sure. You will be a free man soon," he said and left the room. After the door was locked Yakub closed his eyes and thanked God for everything. He went back to the bucket of water for performing his ritual bath.

Epilogue

Three months later

"It was his first night in solitary confinement. The place smelled like dead decomposing matter. The confinement room had just one small window with iron bars. It was one of the darkest nights of the season and Velu tried to sleep in his cell for the rest of his life. He could not find any peace as his eyes fluttered restlessly. Suddenly he opened his eyes and looked towards the window. A shadow fell on his scarred face. With the bright moon in the background, the crow was standing on the sill of the window, just in front of the iron bars."

The audience waited eagerly for the bestselling writer to reveal the ending of the book. There was pin drop silence in the room.

"The crow charged towards the murderer and pecked him for six nights until he developed a severe blood infection.

She wanted him to suffer before he succumbed to his plight," Revati read out from her book, "And on the seventh day, the jail authorities found Velu dead in his room with his wounds rotting. On the window, they found the lifeless body of a crow."

The writer paused to give stress, "Her spirit was set free, she got salvation."

Revati looked up with tears lining up in her eyes. The audience applauded.

Few minutes later, she was taking questions from the audience which consisted of readers, critics as well as reporters.

The first question came from a short man with long hair sitting in the back row with a belly that resembled the rotund of the Taj Mahal's dome. "Revati Krishna…" he said, "I hope you are still selling the movie rights of this book to me!"

"Of course, Mr Kashyap!" she replied to the noted filmmaker and smiled.

Then one of the reporters asked, "Ma'am… Usually writers begin their stories either from the middle or the beginning. Why did you choose to begin from the end?"

Revati thought for a moment and then replied, "This is based on a true story, and everyone knows how it ended, don't they?" she looked at the reporter who was nodding in agreement. Revati continued answering, "What no one knows is how it led to the end. And that's exactly what is in this book… And that's why it is special…"

Revati waited for the next question.

"Ma'am, is it true that the spirit of Parvati guided you to the killer?" one of the readers asked a question that everyone wanted to know about.

"I am sure you will find out when you read this book..." she answered strategically.

Revati looked at her watch and realized that it was time to break the session. She missed the presence of her husband who would always ask the last question.

There was a woman in white jacket sitting next to Vishu. Revati smiled because it was her sister trying to pitch in by raising her hand to ask her question.

"You were going through a tough time after your accident... How did this story help you overcome it?" asked Ruchika.

"I had lost my faith in life... in God. But the story of Parvati and Yakub... it gave me a new purpose in life. And it helped me come back stronger than ever..."

'So, finally have you moved on from the genre of romance... to that of thriller?" asked Vishu.

"This book is dedicated to the memories of my husband. He wanted me to write a thriller and I tried it. But if you read it carefully, you'll know that it is essentially a love story of two fateful people."

Revati inhaled deeply and continued, "In fact, everyone had the same version of the story; the media, the lawyers, the courts, the police. The version where Yakub was the culprit. What I tried was to bring out," the queen of romance novels paused to look at the cover of her book and read out slowly, *"the other side of her story."*

● ● ●